GOD
THE ULTIMATE AUTOBIOGRAPHY

GOD
Ultimate
THE AUTOBIOGRAPHY

Salem House Publishers
Topsfield, Massachusetts

First published in the United States
by Salem House Publishers, 1988
462 Boston Street, Topsfield, MA 01983.

First impression 1987
Copyright © 1987 Jeremy Pascall
Illustrations © 1987 Katherine Lamb

ISBN 0-88162-292-3

DEDICATION

This book is dedicated to Noah.
Who begat Ham, Shem and Japhet.
And Japhet begat Magog, Madai, Javan, Tubal,
Meshech, Tiras and Gomer.
And Gomer begat Ashkenaz, Riphath and Togarmah.
And Togarmah begat Seba, Havilah, Sabtah,
Raamah, Sabtecah and Kevin.
And Kevin begat Wayne, Shane, Duane and Rover.
And Rover begat Alan, Merrill, Jay, Donny and
Little Jimmy.
And Little Jimmy begat Michael, Jermaine, Jackie,
Marlon and Tito.
And Tito begat Groucho, Chico, Harpo, Zeppo,
Gummo and Omo.
And Omo begat Brillo, Brasso, Glitto and Liquid
Gumption.
And Gumption begat John, John, John, John, John,
John and Kenneth, also known as John.
And Kenneth, also known as John, begat John-John.
And John-John begat John-Paul.
And John-Paul 1 begat John-Paul 2, George-Paul
and Ringo-Paul.
And Ringo-Paul begat Gordon, George, Jackie,
Bobby, Bobby, Alan, Geoff, Roger, Martin and Nobby.
And Nobby begat Sidney.
And Sidney didn't begat anybody because he had a
very close friend called Big Gordon.
But Big Gordon begat Huey, Dewey and Louey.
And Louey begat Andrew, Lloyd and Webber.
And Webber begat 'Jesus Christ Superstar' and never
paid Me any royalties.

Introduction

should have thought this is the one autobiography that needs no introduction. After all, everyone knows who I am. In all due modesty – and I'm nothing if not modest, which is not easy when you're the Supreme Being – I must be the most famous person in the entire fifteen universes.[1]

Is there anyone who hasn't heard of Me in one of My many forms? With My colossal following this book is bound to be the greatest thing since sliced manna and yet the publishers – oh, they of little faith! – felt some words of introduction were necessary and implied that

---

1. This is the first indication we have had that there is more than one Universe. Either this is a divine revelation or The Author is prone to exaggeration, a trait frequently found in the extremely aged.

if I didn't supply them they'd ask someone else to write a foreword.

The name mentioned was Johnny Carson, who is apparently the second most famous person after Me. I, of course, objected. If anyone is going to do it, it has to be God and not someone who thinks he is Me.

I've encountered this sort of thing before; a film was made about Me – *Oh, God!* – and without any consultation they cast someone called George Burns as Me. I do object to being played by an actor who is actually older than I am. Or, at least, *looks* older. I was so annoyed I nearly phoned Interfauna to order them to send down a plague of locusts.

So, rather than have someone speak on My behalf I have graciously consented to write this brief introduction with the help of My holy ghost writer.

Do you know the most asked question in history? Of course you don't because you're not omniscient and I am. All-knowing, all-seeing, that's Me. Keep that in mind if you're thinking of stealing this book.

The most asked question in history is this: Does God exist? And my answer? Do I exist? Is the Pope Catholic? Well, as it turns out, he is. Which is a shock because he was supposed to be Jewish. A massive foul-up while I wasn't watching. But I can't be everywhere, can I? All right, I *can* but it's very tiring when you get to My age. Which you won't.

I most certainly *do* exist. Who else do you think created the Earth and every thing that's on it? Martians? Even assuming they did, who do you think created Martians? And who do you think wiped them out after they got too big for their boats?[2]

It is precisely because I do exist that in My infinite wisdom (and please note I am the only person who can

9

truly claim His wisdom is infinite), I have decided to write this book.

You will be aware that the last book about Me is the biggest seller in the history of the world. It would have been the biggest in the history of the fifteen universes but there are many things you don't know, including the fact that in a galaxy as yet undiscovered by Homo Sapiens another of my books – *God on Gardening* – has outsold even The Bible.[3]

I felt it was time The Bible was put into its proper context. It's a good book, in fact it's *The* Good Book, but it was only a biography, and an *unauthorized* one at that. I didn't even write it. In fact, God knows how many people did and even I've forgotten. With such a large team of authors, inaccuracies are bound to creep in and I will correct them in the course of this, definitive, work.

Furthermore, I'm not sure it depicted Me in My best light. For most of the Old Testament I'm made out to be a bad-tempered geriatric who went around visiting boils and pestilence on all-and-sundry. The fact is I'm a Merciful God, sometimes *too* merciful considering what I've let you get away with. I mean, inventing the barbecue is one thing, but testing it on poor Joan of Arc is quite another.

2. This is not a misprint. The Author reveals that the life-form He created on Mars had exceptionally large feet, so large that they wore small ships on them and thus travelled along the Martian canals. The Author wiped them out in a fit of pique because, He contends, walking on water is reserved only for His son.

3. *God on Gardening* is not currently available. It is hoped that this work and its companion volume – *God Housekeeping – How To Have a Heavenly Home* – will be published in the near future.

JOAN OF ARC

BURNT AT THE STEAK (WELL DONE)

And, let's face it, parts of The Bible are terribly boring – all that dreary business of who begat whom, it reads like the Israelite telephone directory – and there's hardly a joke in it. What most people don't realize is that I have a highly developed sense of humor. Why else do you think I created the Belgians?

Taking all this into consideration, I decided it was time I wrote My version of the facts, just to put the record straight, correct the many errors and cover some omissions, not least the matter of The Eleven Commandments which I will come to in due course.

In the meantime, one word for any atheists among you: wrong.

THE AUTHOR OF ALL CREATION

CHAPTER ONE

In The
Beginning ...

n most autobiographies the subject starts at the beginning, but in My case that's tricky. I have no beginning. And, for that matter, I have no end. I'm Infinite. So it makes starting the story difficult. Not to mention ending it. In theory this book could continue indefinitely, which, of course, raises practical difficulties like the immense size of it and the fact that no one would live to read it all the way through. Except Me and that narrows its commercial appeal.[4]

4. It was only with the greatest difficulty that we dissuaded The Author from His original intention of having the entire book inscribed on tablets of stone. While agreeing that this would be a considerable deterrent to shoplifters, we had to point out it would also discourage potential purchasers. He relented when He recalled the damage caused by the two tablets He handed down to Moses, causing the prophet to wear a surgical truss for the rest of his life.

To start as near to the beginning as I can, I wasn't actually born. I just *was*. I still am. I always have been and I always will be. Being Immortal is very nice in most respects – I don't have to worry about things like bus passes and pension plans – but being Infinite has its drawbacks. For example, time has no meaning; I can be idly day-dreaming and suddenly realize that most of recorded history has passed without My even noticing. Suddenly I have to zoom back through the centuries to where I am supposed to be. As a result I always seem to be running about two hundred years behind schedule and this unpunctuality makes life – or, to be precise, after-life – difficult for members of My staff who never know when I'm going to turn up for a meeting. But, as I always say, What's a millennium between friends? And they always laugh. When you're God you' find your little jokes go down rather well.

The other drawback to being Infinite is that I have so much to remember. Most people have trouble remembering what they did yesterday, but not only do I have to remember what happened yesterday, I've also got to remember what's going to happen tomorrow. For example, is the world due to end? And if so, which world? There are, after all, 7,946,587,632 of them. That was at the last count. By the time you read this there may be a few more. Or perhaps several less. And one of them might be your Earth. (That's one of My little jokes, and very funny too. If the destruction of your Earth really was imminent I'd hardly be publishing this, would I? The ways in which I move, My wonders to perform, may be mysterious but they're not stupid.)

So, now, perhaps you can appreciate some of the problems of being Infinite and how it makes starting a book difficult. However, I know that you'd like Me to start the story where it concerns you. Or, rather, your microscopic little planet which, though I say it Myself, is one of My better creations. I particularly like the color scheme, all those greens and blues. Very restful, don't you think? So much nicer than the orange and cerise I used for Dandropy (thirty-ninth galaxy of the fourth universe – turn left after Nibolt and ask again).

I suppose you're surprised that I didn't create your planet first, typical of human egotism. But if it helps, yours was the first planet I created in your galaxy of your universe.

If you've read your Bible carefully – which you haven't, have you? – how many of The Eleven Commandments can you recite? Exactly! You're stuck after "Thou Shalt Not Commit Adultery", aren't you?

All right, even if you've only skimmed The Bible, looking for the rude bits like The Whore of Babylon, you'll know that it starts with Genesis.[5]

The first words of Genesis are: "In the beginning God created the heaven and the earth."

This is true in so far as it goes. Certainly I created Heaven first because I wanted somewhere to live. I can't tell you how boring it used to be just wandering aimlessly through the chartless void, with nobody to talk to, nothing much to do and nowhere to call home. So I decided to create a place to live which would be My idea of ... well ... heaven.

I know you mortals are fascinated by what Heaven is really like, probably because most of you won't see it, unless you repent the error of your ways

---

5. The Whore of Babylon can be found in Revelations xvii-xix, but you're going to be disappointed.

and pretty damn quick. To satisfy your idle curiosity I'll tell you that it has the best of everything – delicious food, magnificent wine, a superb climate and beautiful vistas on every side. A bit like France. But without the French. Not that I'm prejudiced – some of My best saints are French.

So I created this little place. Nothing too ostentatious – just somewhere to hang My halo, as it were. Although don't take this halo business too literally, I obviously don't wear it all the time. It might look good in portraits but, take it from Me, having a light blazing over your head gives you a frightful migraine. Not to mention its effect on others. Look what it did to Saul on the road to Damascus – blinded the poor guy.

Mind you, a halo has its practical uses when one is venturing into the dark abyss of measureless Space to do odd jobs. It does leave both hands free to get on with the work and came in very useful when I decided to create your Earth.

That project came about because, frankly, I was bored. When you have limitless powers you want to try them out, see what you can do with them, maybe create the odd solar system here and there. And then, if the whim takes you, use the stars for juggling practice. Although the fun went out of juggling when I dropped a particularly large asteroid on My toe. It wasn't until then I realized I suffered from bunions. In fact, it wasn't until then that I realized I'd created bunions. Still can't imagine why I did.

Looking through My scrap-book I see that Prototype XI was an interesting experiment. It looked absolutely marvelous with its seventeen oceans, the problem was its shape. Being square the oceans kept slopping over the sides and dripping through Space

until they rained on to Prototype VII. This in itself would not have been a disaster if it wasn't for the extremely low temperatures of Outer Space. Sadly, Prototype VII was destroyed when it was hit by a hailstone three times its own size.

Then there's Prototype XIII. I think I must have been going through My Henry Moore period. Not a great success. Still, nothing's wasted, it proved to be a useful model for Gruyère cheese.

There were other experiments: Prototype XXI was My first attempt at creating a planet with its own life-form. Never having made a life-form before I didn't know what to use as My model. You probably know that Man was created in My own image. But I am ever-changing, I can adopt whatsoever form I like – worth remembering the next time you feel like crushing an ant; it can come as a nasty surprise when an insect turns you into a pillar of salt.

The week in which I created Adam and Eve I just happened to be in the form of a bipedal anthropoid and used that as My template. Rather crude, admittedly, and not particularly beautiful but good enough for you. However, when I was fashioning the creatures on Prototype XXI, I had assumed a completely different form. And, frankly, although lawnmowers are pleasing in their way, they aren't particularly successful as humanoids and an absolute disaster when it comes to procreation.

But I see you're getting restless and want Me to describe the creation of your own piffling little Earth. That's the trouble with you anthropoids, you're so impatient; if you took things a little slower and thought a bit longer you could have avoided so much unpleasantness. Sometimes I wonder why I bother with

creatures who consider the peak of their civilization to be the bedside radio alarm clock with snooze button facility.

Be that as it may, having practiced on other planets, I thought I had ironed out most of the problems when I finally turned My attention to Earth ...

CHAPTER TWO

Monday And Tuesday ... And Earth was Created

I created the Earth and all that's upon it in six days. No, that's not quite accurate; for most of the first twenty-four hours I was working in the dark – except for the glow from My halo – because I hadn't yet invented the day. Well, it stands to reason, doesn't it? To have day you've got to have daylight. And to have daylight you've got to have a sun.

So first I had to create the sun. I said: "Let there be light!" And there was light! Eventually. It took a while. As even you may know, the sun is a ball of burning gas. And you know how difficult it can be to light the gas at the best of times. Imagine what it's like when you haven't yet invented matches, or even fire? So I had to start from scratch and that took a bit longer than I expected and set My plans back, so I put myself on overtime and created the Earth and all that's on it in six days *and* six nights and gave Myself a hernia in the process.

The Bible makes it all sound so simple. "And God said, 'Let there be firmament'." And, according to The Bible, in a twinkling, there was firmament. Balderdash! For a start, I don't use words like "firmament", I'm a plain-speaking God who believes in calling a spade a spade, and a sky a sky.

What I actually said was: "Let there be thingy." Because I hadn't yet got around to giving the bits of the Earth any names; that came a lot later and it wasn't Me who decided that the bit above your head would be called "sky", it was Adam. I wanted to call it "waxtl" but the fool couldn't get his tongue round it, because he had his mouth stuffed full of apple. But that's another story and we'll come to it later.

After some trial and error – it being Monday and Me never being quite at My best on a Monday morning – I created the waxtl (I still think it's a better name than "sky") and looked through my color charts to select a blue which was striking without being garish and then dotted it around with some fluffy yellow clouds. Yes, yellow. Complete disaster! Could have got away with it had the yellow been pastel, but being inexperienced I chose a shade that was sudden to the point of stridency. Used it later for canaries. On them it looks good, but on clouds ... hopeless! In the end, I took the line of least resistance and settled for white.

So that was the sky done and already a whole day had passed. The very first day and not a bad one, all things considered, even though I was slightly behind schedule.

Tuesday morning, I was up with the lark. Or

would have been had I created the lark but birds weren't on My list until Thursday afternoon. According to My diary, the first thing I made on Tuesday morning was breakfast, another first and something of an accident. I was fiddling around with a little model of the planet and thought it looked good enough to eat. So I ate it. Delicious! Inventing breakfast is a splendid way to start the day.

After satisfying the inner God, I turned My attention to the Earth.

If you believe The Bible – and I'm not saying you shouldn't believe it, just don't take it too literally – I merely clicked My fingers and created the Earth. As simple as that!

Again, I'm not saying I can't just click My fingers and an earth will appear – after all, I *am* The Supreme Being – but as we say up here, "The impossible we can do immediately, miracles take a little longer"; rather witty, don't you think? Of course you do. I had it printed on a little wooden plaque and nailed on the wall, next to another saying, "You don't have to be God to work here, but it helps."

Finger-clicking is all very well in theory, but in practice a bit of thought has to go into the ordering of an earth. And especially what you call The Earth. I didn't want to order the wrong model. For example, you wouldn't like to live on a flat Earth, would you? Apparently, some of you seem to think you do, but then some of you might prefer bright yellow clouds – there's no accounting for taste.

After much thought I decided on a round planet, which solved the messy problem of the oceans spilling all over the universe, deterred idiotic flat-earthers from attempting to hurl themselves off the edge to prove their point and had the added advantage of being easily rolled around your universe. And that's no small concern, as I nearly ruptured Myself trying to shift Prototype XXXV from one part of a galaxy to another. For some reason that escapes Me, I'd shaped it like a Chesterfield sofa and had omitted to give it castors. You know, sometimes I wonder whether I'm the right God for the job.

Having finally decided on the shape, I looked at the size. I didn't want it to be too big – there's nothing more vulgar than an oversized planet – but at the same time I wanted something roomy enough to take different styles of continents, a long, thin one here, contrasting with a boxy one there. And having made My mind up about that, I was ready to roll up My sleeves and get down to work.

Looking at your Earth now, I don't think I gave it enough time. Frankly, it was a rushed job and mistakes were made. After all, nobody's perfect. No, that's not true; *I* am perfect but even I can find room for improvement, something the Pope would do well to remember. Theologically speaking, he is infallible but what do you make of a pontiff who goes around kissing airport runways and names himself after two of the Beatles? And the wrong two at that. Personally, I always preferred George-Ringo as a name, but would he listen to Me?

I digress. All-in-all, the Earth turned out pretty well but I realize with hindsight that it leaves something to be desired. The Sahara Desert, for example. It's much too large; a bit of sand is nice but I think I should have been content with the Gobi, neat and compact. The Sahara is definitely overdone. But, of course, it was never meant to be a desert; originally I planned it as

24

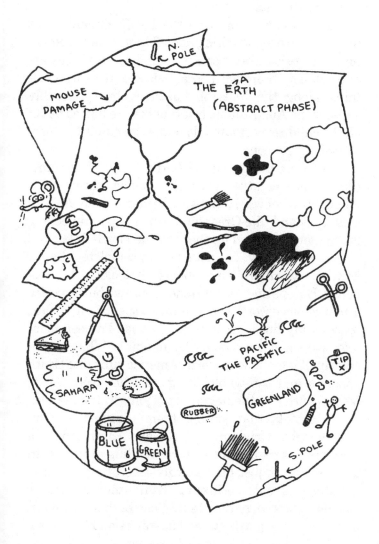

The Milk-And-Honey Theme Park but I spilled coffee on the blueprints.

And speaking of big – the Pacific Ocean! What could I have been thinking about? I must have been in My Blue Period when I created it and got carried away. There's room there for a decent-sized continent, something along the lines of Australia, but preferably without the Australians. Not that I'm prejudiced but of all the children of Adam I do find Australians the most ... well ... raucous.

If I were designing the Earth today, I'd do something more creative with the Pacific, throw in a landmass somewhere between America and Asia, a chunky island like Greenland, which, upon reflection, is completely wasted up there by the North Pole.

Aesthetically, I'm not sure I'm completely happy with the Northern Hemisphere. It looks a bit top-heavy. Europe and Asia do tend to sprawl, but America is marvelous – worth every minute I spent on it; in fact, possibly My finest creation. I just wish I'd been more selective about the people who inhabit it. What I particularly like is the way North America runs into South America and the whole thing stretches from top to bottom with just the narrowest of joins in the middle.

I confess that joining them together was an afterthought. Originally, North and South America were quite separate but as I was fiddling around with the Caribbean, just haphazardly decorating it with a handful of islands, sprinkling them hither and yon as One does, it occurred to Me that one of them would fit perfectly in the gap between Nicaragua and Colombia. And that's how Panama came to be where it is, instead of just off Cuba.

Taking one thing with another, I'm pretty

satisfied with the Earth although I'm well aware that some of you are always whining that it's too small – so ungrateful; I spent an entire week creating your Earth and all you can do is moan. Don't blame Me if it's overcrowded, that's your own fault. You should exercise more restraint in the matter of procreation. If one child is good enough for Me, it should be more than enough for you.

Wednesday
to Friday

o Monday and Tuesday were taken up with creating the waxtl and the planet Earth. On Wednesday I brought forth grasses, herbs, trees and various greengroceries. That was a good day, very enjoyable, but exhausting. Well, you know what hard work gardening can be; just imagine how I felt after creating every single plant from lichen to the California redwood, not to mention roses, nasturtiums, seaweed and the Venus flytrap in between. Even I'm amazed by My achievement but I confess that there were disappointments. Cacti, for example; I never really got them right. Can't imagine what I meant them to look like, but certainly they turned out wrong.

Maybe I had the plans upside down. Anyway, too late to worry now.[6]

That brings Me to Thursday. What happened on Thursday? Well, according to The Bible, I created the sun, the moon and the stars, but that can't be right because I distinctly remember doing the sun first thing on Monday morning. And, splendid though the moon may be, I surely didn't spend an entire day making it. When all's said and done and when poets have finished rhapsodizing over its silver luminescence – a most pleasing effect, to be sure – the moon is just an empty lump of rock which I could have knocked out in any idle moment.

Frankly, I've never understood why you anthropoids have spent so much time, energy and money trying to get to your moon; it isn't worth the trip. And you're going to be terribly disappointed when you eventually reach some of the other planets, although Pluto is quite interesting, being the home of the biggest creature I ever created, the Glarriper. An interesting beast with some remarkable mating habits. But, enough! I don't want to spoil the surprise.

I'm sure I didn't spend a whole day creating the moon and, by the same token, the stars couldn't have taken very long. They look like they were thrown together before breakfast, just sprinkled at random through Space. If I had taken any time over them, I'd have arranged them into some more interesting patterns. There's a lot you can do with stars when you put

6. Interestingly, cacti are omitted from The Author's book, *God on Gardening*. However, He does include an entry on Accountants, which He seems to think are some form of vegetable. Whether this is a mental aberration due to age is unclear.

30

your mind to it. I recall another galaxy in which I arranged them so that if you draw imaginary lines between them they spell out a message. I wish I'd done the same for you, so that every time you gazed up at the night waxtl you'd see:

"God Says: The Meek Shall Inherit The Earth, So
    Don't Let Estate Agents Con You Out Of It."

No, if My memory serves Me correct, and of course it does, I only spent a couple of hours on Thursday throwing bits of rock around the waxtl. The rest of that day and all of Friday were devoted to making animals.

Thursday and Friday were two of the most interesting days of My whole infinite existence. I like animals – in many ways I prefer them to humans. They don't get ideas above their station, they don't complain and they don't talk back.

I never hear rhinoceroses moaning on at Me about the way they look. Your average rhino is quite happy with the way I created him; he doesn't think it odd to have a horn sticking out of his nose. Mind you, he doesn't realize that it was left over from the prototype of a cockroach eight foot high. No, rhinos don't complain, mostly, I suppose, because your average rhino doesn't have much in the way of a brain.[7]

7. It seems The Author designed several beasts that never got off the drawing board. The Giant Cockroach is but one example. There was also a large carnivorous gerbil and a type of warthog which was so outstandingly ugly that even warthogs of the opposite sex would have refused to mate with it, causing it to become extinct within one generation. Additionally, He intended a species of boneless fish. Despite its obvious advantages of being much easier to eat without the risk of choking and saving considerable time in restaurants while waiters make a mess of filleting, The Author never managed to solve the inherent structural problem of an animal that was so floppy it couldn't swim or breathe.

Admittedly, the rhino has more brain than, say, an Afghan hound. Of all My myriad and wondrous creations the Afghan is probably the most stupid (with the obvious exception of the guinea pig. And politicians, but I can't be blamed for them. Entirely the fault of evolution. Or lack of it.) Simple reason, really; I fashioned the Afghan for speed and beauty. Aerodynamically speaking, it is a triumph – just look at that wedge-shaped head, almost no wind-resistance at all. But the trouble is, it's so compact that I left very little room for any cranial matter; consequently the Afghan hound has a tiny brain producing a minuscule I.Q. which is barely matched by that of the people who own it.

Of all My works the brain must be My highest achievement. Only I – and I speak with as much modesty as an omnipotent being can muster – only I, could have conceived of it. But it is so complex that even I encountered problems. For example, early brains weren't altogether reliable. To be brutally frank, some were a complete disaster.

Take the dinosaurs – magnificent beasts in most respects but seriously under-powered in the head department. I underestimated the damage that several tons of flesh and muscle could wreak on a virgin planet when guided by a brain that even the dimmest worm would have found wanting.

Hence the downfall of the dinosaurs. First they started eating all the greengroceries I had provided – even the cacti, which gives some measure of exactly how dense they were – and when they'd denuded the place of comestible vegetation, they started eating each other. And when they ran out of other dinosaurs, they ate themselves. There were few more fearsome sights

33

than to witness a Tyrannosaurus Rex eating its own tail and hind legs and gnawing halfway through its stomach before its brain finally realized it was eating the very thing it was supposed to be filling.

I notice that current scientific thought suggests that the dinosaurs became extinct through evolution, but the fact is the silly brutes destroyed themselves through devolution and actually disappeared up their own alimentary tracts. Never thought of that, did you, Darwin? There's still a lot you anthropoids can learn.[8]

I created all the fishes of the sea and the beasts of the field, including the creeping and crawling things – in fact, everything from the aardvark to the zorro – during most of Thursday and all of Friday. And yet people still don't believe I did it. People still ask, "Did God really create every living creature, including the creeping and crawling things, in a couple of working days?" Did I? Do birds fly? Well, yes they do, which explains why it took Me so long.[9]

Originally I intended pigs to fly. There was nothing intrinsically difficult in this, at least not for Me, it was just a question of making the wings big and powerful enough. In fact, I had several flocks of them fluttering quite successfully, after I'd nudged them out of the trees, but I hadn't realized that the poor creatures

8. When asked about evolution, The Author said it was a mistake and that Charles Darwin should have been a stick insect. A slightly enigmatic answer, possibly one of The Author's celebrated jokes. However, He did add: "Given the choice, would you prefer to think you are descended from Me or an orangutang? But before you answer, consider this: how do you know that I'm not an orangutang?"

9. The zorro is a South American fox-like wild dog. One can't help feeling The Author is showing off His knowledge.

suffer terribly from vertigo. No head for heights, and so, in My infinite mercy, I excused them from flying duties and instead strapped wings on some dull little animals I'd made earlier. Birds turned out rather well, all things considered. Unfortunately, as I'd left it until late in the day, I couldn't get round to converting all of them to flight and so the ostrich never got off the ground. Just as well, really. Imagine a flock of them flying overhead and defecating on everything beneath. You'd be up to your knees in the stuff.

By Friday night I was ready for My bed. After saying My prayers and thanking Myself for My many gifts, I gratefully put My head on My pillow and prepared for another day. And I needed My sleep because Saturday was going to be The Big One.

CHAPTER FOUR

Saturday ...
Adam

aturday morning I *was* up with the lark, having finally got around to creating it, and had cause to regret that I didn't design some form of volume control into it.

Having washed and dressed in My overalls – contrary to what you see depicted on the Sistine Chapel ceiling, I don't always wear a white robe, making worlds is a mucky business – I set out to survey all I had created and saw that it was good. In fact, it was damn terrific and the very best part of all was Eden. A little piece of Heaven on Earth.

How can I describe Eden so that you, with your limited intellect, will be able to grasp its beauty? It was, if you like, the first ever Garden Center. It had everything the discerning God could ask and lacked several things that you seem to appreciate in gardens, like plaster gnomes, plastic tables with Martini umbrellas, and dinky bird baths.

The only desirable thing Eden didn't have was staff. Extraordinary, isn't it, but several millennia later you still can't find staff in Garden Centers, and if you do find someone to point you towards the hollyhocks, they've probably only started work that morning and don't know a Sweet William from a pansy. Human evolution isn't all it's cracked up to be.

So there was Eden, measureless acres of perfection, without anyone to till the earth, trim the hedges or dead-head the chrysanths. I needed a part-time gardener and, as they don't grow on trees – although I sometimes wish I'd thought of that method of propagating humans, it would have saved a lot of messy begatting – I had to create someone to take care of the place.

Not just any animal but one which could walk erect and reach up to prune low branches, which had hands dexterous enough to tie back the sweet peas and was strong enough to cart manure across the lawns. In addition, this creature should have enough intellectual capacity to understand and follow simple orders. In short, I needed a modified chimpanzee. (No disrespect to the chimp, which is far too sophisticated to spend its life carting manure around.)

So I picked up a handful of dust, molded it in My hands and made Adam, Yes, it *was* as simple as that. The work of but seconds, using whatever materials were lying around. Surprised? You shouldn't be because, when all's said and done, I was only making someone who could do odd jobs around the garden.

Look at it this way, I'd already put most of My energies into creating the really *important* animals,

EDEN
GARDEN
CENTER

the ones which I'd intended would rule My new planet. Or The Earth, as you call it. Typical human egotism; you call it "Earth" after the stuff beneath your feet but the planet is hardly composed of earth at all. The vast majority of it is ocean and so obviously I'd spent the majority of My time working on the animals that would live in that environment.

Consequently, I'd invented the most intelligent creature in the entire fifteen universes – the dolphin. However, dolphins are so intelligent they quickly realized that running the planet would lead to such evils as tension, stress, ulcers, war and polyester leisure suits and refused to waste their intellect on such trivia.

Instead they sensibly settled for a quiet life of swimming, begatting, eating, begatting, playing, begatting, and performing tricks that seem to entertain the simple-minded descendants of a handyman.

So that's how it happened, I created the first man almost before you could say "Jack Robinson." Not that you would have said "Jack Robinson", because there wasn't anybody of that name around. There was only this over-sized chimp.

I called him Adam, which is a nice enough name – short, easy to remember and rather classier than Sheldon, Darren or Wayne. I did toy with calling him Geoffrey but it doesn't have the same ring. I didn't bother with a surname. No point really, this Adam was hardly going to be confused with any other. Anyway, I'm not sure I approve of all these names, I've only got one and what's good enough for Me should be quite good enough for you. But, to be fair, there is only one of Me, whereas there are far too many of you. Adam's fault, of course, but we'll come to that later.

Having formed Adam from dust, I breathed life into him by blowing into his nose, which wasn't entirely pleasurable as nostrils are far from being the most exquisite part of the human anatomy. He moaned softly, sneezed violently, stirred into consciousness and scratched his groin.

Within seconds of coming to life, Adam, the first man, rose unsteadily to his feet. He blinked, looked around at the perfection that was Eden, then raised his eyes to the heavens and gazed at the shining glory of his Maker. Then the first man uttered the first words ever heard on Earth. He said: "Well, I'll be a horses' ass."

And I replied, "You will be if you don't watch your language."

It was then I wondered whether I hadn't made a terrible mistake. But you know how it is with hired help, you take what you can get and as he was all I had, I set him to work.

It being his first day I started him off on something simple, fruit-picking. I showed him the trees and the fruit hanging from them and in words of one syllable explained what was expected.

Adam listened and nodded and after a lot of head-scratching he uttered his second sentence. I'll never forget those words which I watched him form with painful slowness. "How much," he asked, haltingly, "does the job pay?"

Then I spake and My voice was as an earthquake, shaking the ground beneath his feet and causing a great wind to howl around him: "I am the Lord Thy God. I created you, fashioned you in My own likeness. You will obey My every command, else I'll turn you back into the dust from whence you came."

Whereupon, hearing these words, he threw himself to the ground, cowering and whimpering before My wrath. He looked so abject and miserable that I took pity on him and raised him to his feet. "Look," I said, kindly, "this is the deal: you're in My garden and I pay nothing except the wages of sin. But I am a merciful God; if you do as you are told, keep the place tidy and don't take long lunch hours, I'll allow you to have as much fruit as you can eat. Can't be fairer than that, can I?

"You can eat anything in the garden you like but, take My advice, steer clear of those things lying on the ground, which are stones; and, especially, those things over there which look like stones but are, in fact, rabbit droppings.

"Otherwise, everything in Eden is yours for the taking. Except – and I'll say this once, so listen carefully – *except* the apples from the big tree in the middle of the herbaceous border, just to the right of the snapdragons. Those apples are Mine and Mine alone. Eat one of those and you'll find yourself in big trouble. Understand?"

He nodded mutely.

"Good. Now I've got to go and check whether the Himalayas have set, they were still soft the last time I looked, so you get on with your work. And just remember who's The Boss around here."

And I left him standing there, in the orchard, staring at a pineapple he held in his hand, wondering into which orifice he should insert it.

CHAPTER FIVE

Later The Same Day ... Eve

hen I created Eve I little realized I was also creating feminism. Now I've nothing against feminists, after all I've had enough experience of being a woman to know exactly how they feel. Yes, let's settle this tedious theological debate once and for all. I *am* a woman ... when I want to be.

As I keep trying to remind My clergy, I am The Trinity. But they seem to think that being Three-In-One means I'm some sort of lawnmower oil. Let Me make Myself clear: I am God the Father, God the Son and God the Holy Ghost. And I'm more than that; I am also God the Mother, God the Daughter, God the Niece and God the Second Cousin Once Removed. In brief, I am God the Whatever I Want To Be – male, female, animal, vegetable or mineral – so treat your houseplants, even the cacti, with more respect, because you never know ...

As a woman – when I am a woman – I take great exception to charges of sexism, just because I created Adam before Eve. The explanation is simple. Adam was the prototype, and, frankly, watching him stumbling around Eden, bumping into trees and trying to open a coconut by knocking it vigorously against his forehead, it didn't take Me long to realize that he left plenty of room for improvement.

I decided to have another try. Eve was going to be My masterpiece so I devoted more time to her creation and, of course, I used superior materials. Dust was good enough for Adam but for Eve I worked from living tissues.

As everyone knows, I used one of Adam's ribs. Not, as some think, a spare rib – I was creating life, not testing recipes for a Chinese cookbook.[10]

This was to be My most delicate operation, a pioneering rib transplant. I scrubbed up and prepared to put Adam into a deep sleep – the world's first anaesthetic – but he saved Me the trouble by rendering himself unconscious with his coconut. Then, with utmost care and concentration, I performed the first ribectomy. From that rib came Eve.

And lo! Woman was created.

I gazed upon her and saw she was good. What an improvement! So much better formed, softer, rounder, smoother, with none of those ugly dangly bits which

10. The Author has, in fact written a companion volume to *God on Gardening* called *Kitchen Miracles*, which includes such recipes as "1001 Things To Do With A Pillar Of Salt"; "Feeding 5000 Unexpected Guests On Loaves And Fishes" and "Water Into Wine."

had been causing Adam so much trouble and pain as he'd tried to take a short-cut through the brambles.

Gently I re-awoke Adam and presented Eve to him, saying she was to be his partner and they were to live together and share the work equally and told him to take that silly grin off his face while I was talking to him.

Within that one day I had created Adam and Eve, man and woman, and before long they were doing what man and woman would do throughout history. They were arguing.

Arguing about the correct way to open a coconut. Adam still clung to his theory that the best method was to tap it sharply against the forehead, and in consequence invented the headache. Eve suggested using a rock which, eventually, he did, and came close to pioneering the frontal lobotomy. When he recovered consciousness she indicated that next time he should hit the coconut with the rock. But by then it was late on Saturday night, I was exhausted from My labors and, frankly, fed up with humans.

What I needed was a vacation. And so I created Sunday ...

CHAPTER SIX

Sunday ...
What I Did On
My Vacation

Having labored long and hard, I set aside the seventh day as a day of rest. Ever since, people have speculated on how I passed that first Sunday.

As you might expect, I spent much of the day on My knees. Have you any idea how much mess is left after creating a world? It took Me hours of scrubbing before I got My workroom tidy.

As for what I did during the rest of the day – it's none of your damned business. I'm entitled to my private pleasures like anyone else. So keep your nose out of My affairs.

CHAPTER SEVEN

The Second Week

oke up on Monday with a fearful headache.[11] I made My usual ablutions but decided against shaving, partly because My hand was not as steady as I'd have wished and partly because I wanted to see what I looked like in a beard. One of My better decisions; the beard makes Me look more ... well, Godlike ... in portraits. Though I do wish painters would refrain from depicting Me wearing a flowing robe. Makes Me

11. This may indicate that The Author had inadvertently invented the hangover. In fact, the mother and father of hangovers. And neglected to invent Alka-Seltzer. When questioned on the subject The Author was evasive. He merely muttered "chihuahua." Further research reveals that the chihuahua is the only hairless dog; whether this is a result of an early attempt at curing the hangover must remain speculation.

look as though I've forgotten to change out of My nightshirt. Which is nonsense anyway because I've always favored pyjamas.

Decided to clear My head and have a breath of fresh air by taking a stroll around Eden.

The sun was high in the waxtl. The birds were singing. The trees were in leaf and every plant was blooming, except for the cacti which were being stubbornly prickly.[12]

In the course of My perambulation there was an unfortunate incident; while viewing the cacti and wondering whether it was too late to turn them into something more useful and decorative, like, for example, luxurious reclining garden chairs with detachable, machine-washable chintz covers, I inadvertently trod on the tail of a snake that was basking in their shade. The beast took great exception to this small accident and reacted in what can only be described as a hostile and unforgiving manner. I seem to remember it hissed: "Who do you think you are, God Almighty?" To which I obviously replied, "Yes." Then it said: "In which case, why didn't you give me any legs?" And it slithered away, in high dudgeon muttering darkly to itself and sticking its tongue out in an offensive manner. I sometimes wonder if My small act of carelessness was to have a bearing on subsequent events.[13]

12. The sky was still known as the "waxtl" as Adam had not yet got around to naming his surroundings. There are four possible reasons for this: [a] he hadn't had time; [b] language hadn't been invented; [c] he was too stupid or [d] he was otherwise engaged, as will become apparent.

13. The Author reveals that He now regrets the creation of the snake. He fashioned it before He discovered that He'd used up His remaining stock of legs on the centipede.

I continued My stroll, but of Adam and Eve there was not a sign. Eventually, however, I heard a noise issuing from a clump of blackberry bushes and upon investigating found that within hours of his creation Adam had made two discoveries. The first was begatting and the second was that blackberry bushes are not the ideal places in which to begat.

Obviously I had always intended that humans should begat – Eden was a big garden and would need more hands to tend it, especially if the staff were going to spend their time begatting when they should be spreading the compost – but even I was startled by the rapidity with which Adam (a creature of low intellect who had trouble distinguishing one orifice from another) had found one of the purposes of his ugly dangly bits.

Astonishingly, he was aware of begatting even before the rabbits, both of which, at that point, were too occupied with eating My varied and bounteous green-groceries to turn their minds to other pleasures of the flesh. (Rabbits did not discover begatting for some three weeks when, full to bursting and, perversely, having rejected cacti as a source of food, they explored the possibility of procreation and, like humans, haven't stopped since.)

Although Adam and Eve were the first begatters on Earth, their discovery of the techniques involved came only through trial and error, with Adam doing most of the trying and making most of the errors. But you have to understand this was eons before sex therapists were around to tell him where he was going wrong. And of course, I wasn't inclined to offer any advice as the act of begatting is a matter of indifference to Me. If I feel the need to procreate Myself – which has only occurred once in My infinite existence – I ask the Holy Ghost to see to it on My behalf.[14]

But I digress. I chanced upon Adam and Eve behind this blackberry bush just as he was revealing his great discovery to her. He was, in fact, making excited guttural noises and pointing towards his tumescent nether portions. Eve's reaction was both enthusiastic and swift – she kneed him in the groin. This effectively set back human procreation by several hours and very nearly ended it before it began. In retrospect this may not have been such a bad thing, considering all the problems you humans have caused; if Eve had succeeded in unmanning Adam My creation would have been spared blights like war, torture, nuclear weapons and polyester pants. Sadly, she merely succeeded in cooling Adam's ardor for a short period and forcing his voice up several octaves. An improvement, in My opinion.

Personally, I would like to draw a discreet veil over the development of human begatting, but I am aware it is one of the few topics of interest to most members of your species who have resolutely ignored My Seventh Commandment about not coveting your

14. The question of the Virgin Birth has taxed the finest theological minds – and some bishops of the church – for two millennia. Recent debates about surrogacy have largely ignored the fact that The Author employed not only a surrogate mother but a surrogate father – The Holy Ghost – as well. Atheists have frequently cited the Virgin Mary as an argument against The Author, one recently declaring, "Even if there was a God, would you trust a man who got an unmarried girl pregnant and then tried to blame it on someone else?"

When asked about his view of atheists, The Author replied: "I don't believe in them."

neighbor's ass or, indeed, any other part of his or her anatomy.[15]

I have always thought that the act of begatting is the most ludicrous of human functions. I blame Myself. Had I given it more careful thought I would have designed the entire mechanism differently, probably by eliminating any physical contact. This worked successfully in one of the other universes where I created a single-sex life form that procreated itself by sneezing. This brilliantly simple method worked beautifully for several generations until one great-great-great-grandchild caught a nasty cold, passed it on to its siblings and caused a catastrophic population explosion.

The method I designed for you is much too complicated, appears to be physically uncomfortable (if not, judging from the way some of you do it, downright dangerous) and extremely undignified. I've never understood why it seems to give you so much pleasure. Personally, I prefer a nice cup of tea.

Not that begatting gave Adam much pleasure, at least initially. Having regained his breath, and the lower register of his voice, after his first attempt to introduce Eve to it, he tried again. This time he chose his location more carefully, well away from blackberry bushes, and, after some initial confusion about who was to do what to whom and which organs should go where – a lot of time was wasted as he attempted to whisper seductively into her nose (there were one or two other misapprehensions of a similar nature which I shall not

15. When asked whether Biblical scholars have misinterpreted the Tenth Commandment by implying it means we should not covet our neighbor's donkey, The Author replied: "Donkey? How many people fall in love with donkeys? I thought that sort of thing had died out with Sodom and Gomorrah. Perhaps I didn't use enough brimstone."

elaborate on) – the first human begatting was achieved. This experience left Adam in a state of blissful euphoria and Eve wondering what all the fuss was about.

Nevertheless, they persisted, mostly, I think, because Eve hadn't yet found a grunt that meant "No" and because she was beginning to realize that the first method of contraception was becoming less reliable as Adam became more agile in avoiding the knee in the groin.

Persistence paid off; within a remarkably short time Eve found that begatting was not unpleasant and, indeed, was far more pleasant than the main purpose for which I had put them on Earth – weeding the borders. As I had better things to do than watch the pair of them work through all the possibilities of advanced begatting, I left them to it. After all, they couldn't come to much harm while My back was turned.

CHAPTER EIGHT

The Fall of Man

few days later I was taking a turn round the garden when I became aware that all was not as usual. For a start it was unnaturally quiet. Silence reigned apart from the riffle of the breeze through the leaves, the trilling songs of the birds and the bellow of yet another pain-maddened beast which has tried to browse on the cacti.

It took Me a few moments to realize what was missing – the unmistakable sound of Adam and Eve begatting. No sound at all come from them.

So I called out. But answer came there none. I called again. Still no answer. This was odd. I didn't doubt that they'd heard Me because when I raise My voice it is like unto a great wind that stirs the oceans and causes the mountains to tremble. This, I find, usually catches people's attention.

I called a third time and when the oceans stopped slopping about and the mountains had come to rest, I heard a small cough behind Me. Turning round I saw Adam. And he saw Me. And then he did a most extraordinary thing, he grabbed a handful of leaves and attempted to cover his nakedness. And as I watched he threw himself to the ground at My feet and howled. And I spake gently unto him, saying, "Adam, why did you cover your nakedness? And, more to the point, why did you use stinging nettles?"

But still Adam howled and so I found him a dock leaf and as he applied it to the affected parts, I said, "Adam, you and I are going to have a little chat, man to God. Tell Me, have you eaten of the fruit of the big tree in the middle of the herbaceous border?"

And Adam nodded.

I am, I think you'll agree, a Merciful God.[16]

However, there are certain things up with which I will not put. In the short time since I had created Adam and Eve I had turned a blind eye on their neglect of the Garden Center while they were engaged in their begatting experiments. I had overlooked the weeds in the paths, the untrimmed lawns, not to mention the fact that in the course of their activities they had flattened my best peonies. All this I had let pass.

But there is a point beyond which even I will not go.

I had laid down only one rule when I allowed

16. One would tend to agree that The Author is a Merciful God. Mainly because the last person who disagreed is now a small, rather dull cactus in the middle of the Negev Desert.

Adam the free run of the place – neither he nor his wife were to eat of the fruit from the big tree in the middle of the herbaceous border. I told them quite specifically that this was The Tree of Life.[17]

When I laid down this rule I thought that My order was clearly understood. I did not consider it necessary to nail a notice on the tree saying: "God's Apples! Do Not Eat Or Else!" Or "Thieves Will Be Prosecuted." Mind you, it wouldn't have done any good as Adam and Eve had not yet got around to inventing language – apart from a series of grunts that meant "Do you fancy a bit of begatting?" – let alone mastered reading. At this point in human development if I showed them a notice they'd have attempted to either eat it or use it as an advanced begatting aid. (I suppose it is a measure of human development that if I showed you a notice today you'd print it on T-shirts or buy the video rights.)[18]

I knew as soon as Adam attempted to cover his parts that My order had been disobeyed. Until he had eaten of the fruit of My tree he didn't know he was naked, he didn't know anything much apart from begatting. The only thing he knew – or was supposed to know – was that he shouldn't eat My apples. In fact, he was so ignorant that I was surprised he actually

17. Also known as The Tree of Good and Evil and thought by experts to be a superior species of Golden Delicious.

18. A range of T-shirts will shortly be available, including "God Says ... Repent!". Also watch out for "God: End Of The World Tour" jackets. Video rights are also available, and Andrew Lloyd Webber is bidding to make the musical of the video of the T-shirts. Although The Author is resisting, "I may be Merciful but I find it difficult to forgive what he did to My son's story."

managed to put the apple in his mouth and not some other inappropriate orifice.

What I wanted to know was why Adam had disobeyed Me and after the dock leaf had soothed his pain, he told Me the story.[19]

It seems that Eve had become an enthusiastic begatter, so enthusiastic that Adam started to feel distinctly peaked and moaned piteously every time she nudged him in the ribs. This was partly because he was still recovering from his recent ribectomy, and partly because he was suffering from the world's first double rupture plus multiple lacerations caused by her insistence on trying to begat while hanging upside down from a cactus.

Eve quickly became irritated by his lack of response and took to wandering around Eden to find whether there was anyone else with whom to begat. Having failed in this endeavor, she got bored and tried to discover whether there was anything as good as or better than begatting.

According to Adam, one afternoon in the course of her wanderings she got into idle conversation with a snake who just happened to be hanging around. They chatted about this and that and the snake finally brought the conversation round to the apples on My tree. It seems he managed to persuade her that they had powerful aphrodisiac qualities which would work wonders on Adam's flagging energies. And she was

19. There is some confusion here. The Author has stated that Adam's grasp of language was primitive at best, and yet they conversed. When asked, The Author said they communicated telepathically. "I read Adam's mind, the work of but seconds."

sorely tempted. So she plucked one, took a bite, ran back to her man and told him to eat it.

Adam, being too exhausted to argue, also took a bite and thus committed Original Sin.

Obviously, I had no alternative but to fire Adam and Eve from the Garden Center. Deafening My ears to their pleas, I cast them forth and slammed the gates behind them.

I watched them stumble off, naked and forlorn, and as they entered the wilderness, Adam turned to Me and said, "All of this for one lousy apple! Had I known You'd take this attitude I'd have done something *really* naughty!"

And I spake unto him and said: "This is your punishment for disobeying the word of the Lord Thy God. But what really gets up My nose is that you actually expected me to believe all that rubbish about a talking snake."

CHAPTER NINE

After The Fall ...

fter The Fall came The Winter. And that came as a nasty shock to Adam and Eve because in the Garden Center they'd got used to a warm climate and it took them a while to find some suitable covering for their nakedness. Adam had particular problems and after several experiments with various bits of greengrocery, including holly and poison ivy – which had disastrous effects on his begatting – was set to give up. It was Eve who discovered fig leaves were far less painful. She attempted to attach three of them to her body but they kept falling off. This had a remarkably therapeutic effect on their begatting because every time they fell, Adam felt one of his urges and, consequently, in the spring Eve gave birth to a child.

They called him Cain, not a particularly

attractive name, but he wasn't a particularly attractive child. Perhaps his least attractive trait was his tendency to murder people. To be fair, he only killed one person, his brother Abel (where do they find these names?) but as there were only four people on Earth at the time he did, effectively, remove a quarter of the population, making him, proportionately, the worst mass murderer in all history.

At first Cain pleaded innocent of the crime. Until I pointed out that the list of suspects consisted of three. And two of them, to wit his mother and father, had cast-iron alibis, being engaged, as they were, in populating the Earth, which involved round-the-clock begatting. Faced with this evidence he finally cracked, admitted his crime and entered as mitigation the fact that he came from a broken home. I overruled this on the grounds that, in My opinion, a couple of rocks under a tree didn't constitute a hovel, let alone a home. And anyway, it was only broken because he had smashed it in a fit of temper. He then tried to plead self-defense, claiming that Abel had attacked him with a lupine.

I pointed out that if Cain thought a lupine was a deadly weapon, he'd do better to plead insanity but even that wouldn't get him far because he was as sane as the next man, even given that the next man was Adam. Which wasn't saying much.

I had no choice but to find Cain guilty. My first impulse was to put him on the wrong end of a thunderbolt, but as this would further deplete the population and, because he hadn't tried to blame a snake for his crime, I decided to be merciful and exiled him to The Land of Nod. Wherein he dwelt, tilling the earth and telling anyone he met, "My name's Cain, I'm the world's first murderer. Not many people know that."[20]

In the meantime life outside Eden continued as usual. Adam and Eve multiplied and begat many sons including Seth who was born when they were 130 years old. They also had daughters who are not mentioned at all in The Bible, probably because they were all called Eve except for their last born girl who was given the name Stanley.[21]

For the next eight hundred years all was peace in My Creation. Adam spent his days delving the ground, hewing wood and drawing water and his nights begatting. Sometimes, for a change, he would begat during the day and delve during the night. And, on other occasions, he would attempt to draw wood and hew water. Very occasionally he would attempt to begat with wood. And when he wasn't doing any of that he was teaching his hundreds of children everything he

20. The land of Nod; this does not mean The Author sent him to sleep. Nod was a country East of Eden next to The Land of Wink. For many years the descendants of Cain disputed with the inhabitants of Wink as to which country was the better. Eventually a Nod fought in single combat against a Wink to decide the issue. Unfortunately the Wink turned up drunk – he became known as the first tiddley wink – and was easily beaten. So, contrary to popular belief, a Wink is not as good as a Nod, even to a blind horse.

21. When asked whether Stanley was originally a girl's name, The Author replied: "No. Adam was a good begatter but he was terrible at thinking up names. He also had thirty-two sons and a pet log called Stanley. He befriended a lump of wood and took it everywhere with him. He used to throw dogs for it to fetch and could never understand why it didn't retrieve them. Looking at Adam I'm amazed that the human race ever developed beyond the Stone Age. Frankly, Eve was the brains of the family and it was she who wore the trousers. Mostly because he could never grasp that he shouldn't put both feet into the same leg."

knew, which was not particularly taxing for either him or the children.

And eventually it came to pass that Adam died, at the age of 930, from terminal boredom.

As for Eve, she lived on to see her great-great-great-great-great-great-great-great-great-great-great-great-great-great-great-great-great-grandson, Sheldon, grow to be a man and become the world's first certified vegetable and tax consultant.[22]

After this crushing disappointment she lost the will to live and I carried her off to Heaven where she resides to this day, greeting souls at The Pearly Gates with the words, "I am Eve, the Mother of the Human Race, have some chicken noodle soup. But first, tell me, how come you didn't write?"

22. The Author obviously means he was a certified accountant. See footnote 6.

CHAPTER TEN

Avant Le Déluge[23]

n all the planets in all the galaxies in all the constellations of the fifteen universes I have never created a lifeform so troublesome, quarrelsome and downright disagreeable as you anthropoids on Earth. No sooner have I laid down the Seven Deadly Sins than you've broken them and are committing others that hadn't even occurred to Me. It started early with one of the great-great-great-et cetera-grandchildren of Adam, a nasty piece of work called Mahalameehal. By the time he'd reached puberty he'd got through Pride, Anger, Envy, Lust, Gluttony and Avarice; the only Deadly Sin he hadn't committed was

---

23. Before The Flood. One suspects The Author is showing off again.

Sloth and that was because he was far too busy with the others to be lazy.

I never had these problems with the Zeugons – a nice, peaceable race on the fourth planet to the left of the fifth galaxy of the seventh universe. They are so law-abiding that I only had to give them One Deadly Sin – I expressly forbade them to have carnal knowledge with woodlice. And not one Zeugon ever disobeyed me. The fact that there were no woodlice on Zeugon is beside the point.

Why couldn't you be more like Zeugons? No sooner had Cain committed fratricide than his relatives were indulging in every form of sin, crime, vice and perversion. If I live to be a thousand – which I will and, indeed, have – I will never understand why you couldn't be content with tending your gardens. To an extent I blame myself for not bestowing My own infinite patience on you.

In those early days people lived longer than they do now. Methuselah was the oldest man who ever lived. He was 969 when he died and while that is no great age as compared to Mine, it's a lot for a simple-minded bipedal with a low boredom threshold.

Not that Methuselah was a sinner, he lived an exemplary life but I felt sorry for him; the poor man was driven to distraction by being constantly asked the secret of his longevity. And having to repeat time and again that he put it down to the complete absence of cigarettes, alcohol, high cholesterol food and traffic accidents. His was a sad death, he was burned to a cinder attempting to blow out all the candles on his 970th birthday cake.

Most of his contemporaries, faced with years and years of nothing much to do – and yet knowing that however long they lived they'd never survive to see the introduction of the video recorder, personal stereo or vibro-massager – made their own entertainment such as theft, mugging, arson and rape.

To be absolutely honest – and I can't be anything else – although I was vaguely aware of their hobbies I'd rather neglected Earth. I think I must have taken forty winks one afternoon and woke to discover that several hundred years had passed and that things had got out of hand.

I am not easily shocked – after all, there is nothing I haven't seen – but looking down upon the Earth I was shaken by the evil I perceived in the hearts of men. The whole planet was populated by villainy and corruption, My glorious Creation was besmirched and soiled. Sin of every type flourished and wickedness reigned throughout the lands of the world. The entire globe was like one enormous Las Vegas, but without its hideous neon signs. Even this did nothing to mollify Me.

I was moved to great wrath and I said to Myself: "I will destroy man whom I have created from the face of the Earth; both man, and beast, and the creeping thing, and the fowls of the air; for it repenteth me that I have made them." Actually, that's what the scribes who wrote The Bible say I said. A bit florid because they liked to make Me sound pompous, which I'm not. In fact, My own phrase was rather pithier but the gist was the same. I decided to wipe the whole lot out and start again. Now, you see, I've admitted I made a mistake – not easy for a Supreme Being – and would a pompous God do that?[24]

24. "The creeping thing." Most scholars interpret this as referring to the snake. But, as we shall see, The Author was referring to the quug.

Having decided to exterminate all these humans and beasts and fowls, not to mention the creeping thing, I had to decide how best to effect their removal. My preference has always been for the judiciously targeted Intercontinental Ballistic Thunderbolt; as a long-range weapon it can hardly be equalled – it's quick, it's clean and it's accurate. Well, mostly it's accurate, occasionally there's a small mishap – I remember doing some target practice over the barren wastes of North America and I slightly misjudged the power of My bolt. Unfortunate, but I'm told the Grand Canyon is now very popular with tourists.

However, the thunderbolt is only really effective against individual targets, one miserable sinner picked out among a crowd. Tremendously impressive, it puts the fear of Me into any spectator. But for the task in hand I needed something that would wipe out hundreds of thousands and frankly I didn't have the time or the inclination to pick them off one at a time.

The obvious answer was something that would cover the whole Earth and do the job in one fell swoop. Something a bit classier than a plague of boils but not as ostentatious as a full-scale holocaust, which leaves the most appalling mess to be cleared up. Looking at My arsenal, I finally decided on rain.

As I think I may possibly have mentioned before, I am a Merciful God.[25] And so before I turned on the taps I thought I'd give the world one more chance. Frankly, I slightly regretted My hasty decision to wipe every living thing off the face of the Earth – the beasts and the fowls and even the creeping thing had done nothing to

---

25. The Author has, in fact, mentioned this before. And one is still inclined to agree with Him.

offend Me and the various greengroceries were utterly innocent, even the cacti had their good points![26]

If I destroyed them I'd only have to go to all the bother of creating them again. So I decided to have a quick look to see if there was any human worth sparing.

Which is how I found Noah. He was just an ordinary chap but he'd lived a good, honest life with his wife, Norah. If I have one criticism of him it is that at the age of five hundred he'd only fathered three children which shows that he and Norah hadn't been doing their share of begatting but nobody's perfect, except Me, and apparently Norah Noah was a martyr to migraines, which must have cramped his style somewhat. Also, although it was regrettable that they'd named their offspring Japhet, Shem and Ham, I couldn't really count this a sin. Still, I do think Ham is a damned stupid name and later I prohibited the Children of Israel from having anything to do with it. Typically, they went too far and wouldn't even eat the stuff.

I looked into Noah's heart and saw it was pure and I decided that he and his little family would be spared the inundation. So, one evening, as he was cultivating his garden while most of the neighbors were out enjoying themselves at the Rape, Loot And Plunder Club – it was, if I recall, their Strip Bingo and Ladies' Pillage Night – I spake gently unto Noah, not wishing to alarm him.

"Noah", I spake, "This is The Lord Thy God!"

But answer came there none.

And again I spake unto him, saying, "Noah, I am The Lord Thy God!"

26. It seems The Author is making a joke. And a very funny one too. Remember, being turned into a cactus is even less amusing.

Still no answer. And yet a third time I spake: "Noah! This is the Lord Thy God speaking."

And this time Noah looked up and beheld Me and he spake unto Me saying, "I don't know who you are but you'll have to speak up because I'm a bit deaf."

So I raised My voice slightly, but not so much as to start the oceans slopping and the mountains trembling or so that we could be overheard by any busybodies. And I spake unto him again saying, "Noah, I am The Lord Thy God, do you understand what I am saying unto you?"

And Noah looked up again and spake, saying, "About half-past-six. Sorry I can't be more accurate than that but the digital watch hasn't been invented yet."

And once more I spake, louder this time, saying "I'm not asking you the time. I'm telling you that I am The Lord Thy God!"

And Noah said, "All right, you don't have to shout. If there's one thing I can't stand, it's people who go around acting as though they're God."

And that is when, in My infinite wisdom, I decided that Noah could drown with the rest of them.

CHAPTER ELEVEN

The Ark

'm not sure if I've mentioned this before, but if I'm nothing else, I am a Merciful God. Having left Noah to his fate I fell to pondering that I'd been a trifle impatient with him. After all, a certain deafness is only to be expected in a 500-year-old man. As I get older I, Myself, find it harder to hear everything that's said to Me. I do wish you wouldn't mumble when you say your prayers, it makes My job so much harder. Not that many of you do say your prayers any more; unless you're really in trouble and then you can't get on your knees fast enough, can you? Well, I do object to being treated like some cosmic insurance policy – you don't like paying your premiums, but you're quick enough to call on Me when something goes seriously wrong. The next time you want My help, I suggest you read the

69

small print – especially the clause that refers to "Act of God" and which states that God will only act if you're fully paid up. Or, rather, fully prayed up![27]

Where was I? Ah, yes, Noah. I reconsidered My rather hasty decision and gave him another chance. So I returned the next evening and before attempting to communicate with him again I blew in his ear and cured his deafness.[28]

And I spake unto him saying, "Noah, can you hear Me?"

And he jumped out of his seat and said, "Oh! My God! You scared me half to death."

And I said "Yes, Noah, I *am* your God."

He said, "Pull the other one, it's got bells on it."

And I looked around and saw neither bells nor anything to pull. And I said, "You speak in riddles, Noah. Look at Me and be not afraid."

And Noah looked at Me and gazed upon My majesty and said unto Me, "I truly believe you are God."

And I said to him, "Yes, Noah, I am."

And he said, "Somehow I thought You'd be taller."

And I told him My intentions: "I am sickened by the depravity that stalks My Creation and I have decided to wash it all away. Shortly there will be torrential rains that will last for forty days and forty nights and will cause a great flood that will cover the Earth. And everything upon the face of the Earth will

27. Another example of The Author's highly developed sense of humor.

28. In the light of what The Author has written about His own partial hearing loss, the editor asked Him why He didn't perform a similar miracle on Himself. He replied: "A miracle is one thing, but have you ever tried blowing in your own ear?"

be destroyed. Everything, that is, except you and your family."

And Noah looked at Me and said, "Rain? We never get rain in these parts at this time of year."

And I scowled at Noah and he, seeing My displeasure, said, "All right, keep Your halo on. You're the boss, if You say it's going to rain, that's fine by me. So what do You want me to do?"

And I told him. And when I had finished, he spake unto Me, saying: "Let's see if I've got this right. You want me to build an ark 300 cubits long by 50 cubits wide by 30 cubits high, made of best quality gopher wood and lined inside and out with pitch. Is that correct?"

"Yes, Noah, that is correct."

And Noah said, "Fine. I can't see any problems. Apart from the fact that I can't even put up a shelf straight. And that my garden, in which You want me to build this bloody great boat, is only 20 cubits long and 15 cubits wide. And that I, a 500-year-old man with a bad back, am supposed to do all this single-handed, without help from anyone.

"I don't suppose it ever occurred to You, in Your infinite wisdom, to give the job to a firm of professional boat-builders?"

And I spake unto him, saying, "I have chosen you, Noah, for this task. I will give you the strength and skill to complete the work. Have faith in Me. Did I not cure you of your deafness?"

And Noah looked up at Me and spake unto Me, saying, "Pardon?"

And I was sorely vexed by Noah until he said, "It was just a joke. Haven't You got a sense of humor?"

And I laughed and said, "Indeed, I do have a sense

of humor, Noah!" And to prove it, I turned him into a cactus.

Having enjoyed My little joke, I restored Noah to his natural form and he went away rejoicing. He ran to his wife saying, "Norah, it is going to rain for forty days and forty nights."

And Norah replied, "Really, dear? Well I expect the garden could do with it."

And then he told her, "And I'm going to build an ark 300 cubits long and 50 cubits wide and 30 cubits high."

And she replied, saying, "That's nice, dear, every man should have a hobby."

And Noah said, "You don't understand, I have been vouchsafed this task by God Himself."

And she replied, "Of course you have, dear. Now wash your hands before supper."

And he said, "I'm not even going to bother telling you about the cactus."

CHAPTER TWELVE

Le Déluge[29]

 oah toiled long and hard on the ark. It took him a hundred years, far longer than I had intended but it wasn't his fault, he had to wait seventy years for planning permission from the local council.

As he built it people journeyed from far and wide and marvelled at the structure, saying, "Verily, it is a huge garden shed. When it is finished it will be even bigger than that owned by The Jonahs next door." While others scoffed, saying "Verily, he is only trying to keep up with The Jonahses."[30]

And to those that mocked, Noah merely said,

29. The Flood: when asked why He'd rendered this into French, The Author said, "John-Paul's not the only one who can speak fluently in tongues."

30. "Verily" appears to have been a popular name in those days.

"Sticks and stones may break my bones, but words will never hurt me."

Hearing this, the mockers were amazed and stopped hurling scornful words at him and hurled sticks and stones instead. But still did My good and faithful servant continue with his task, even in bandages.

Eventually it was finished and I made a tour of inspection. I saw that he had made it of good gopher wood, that he had lined it with pitch both inside and out and that, as I had ordained, its dimensions were 300 cubits by 50 cubits by 30 cubits.[31]

I congratulated Noah on his work, saying, "Well done! but why did you paint it bright pink?"

And he said, "That was the wife's idea. Personally I favored something less garish but she insisted that it matched the curtains." And then he said, "Lord, I have built this ark as You ordained, except for the color which I admit is definitely on the lurid side. I have toiled at this task for a hundred years which is a long time and I've completely forgotten what the thing is for."

And again I told him of the great inundation and how the ark would save him and his family from extinction. And he said, "Lord, there is only me and my wife;

31. A cubit was the measure taken from the length of the arm, from the elbow to the tip of the middle finger. It was rather imprecise, ranging from 18 to 22 inches, depending on the height of the workman. Assuming Noah was of average height, the dimensions of the ark would be approximately 150 yards long by 25 yards wide by 15 yards high. Or 450 feet long by 75 feet wide by 45 feet high. Or 137.16 metres long by 22.86 metres wide by 13.72 metres high. On the other hand, The Bible (Genesis vi, 4) states, "There were giants in the earth in those days." So it could have been much bigger. When asked to clarify this point, The Author said, "Who cares?."

our sons, Shem and Japhet and their wives, and their children Sharon, Darren, Karen and Warren. Not forgetting Ham and his wife and their children Bacon, Pork and little Chipolata. This is a very large ark for fifteen people."

And I said, "Noah, do not forget the animals."

And he said, "Animals? What animals? You never mentioned any animals."

And I said, "Well, I thought you had enough to do without worrying about the animals." And I told him of My plan.

And Noah spake unto Me, saying, "Let me see if I've got this right. You want me to travel throughout the known world and catch two specimens of every living animal, one male and one female, from the aardvark to the zorro, whatever they may be. Even though I am allergic to animal fur which brings me out in a plague of boils.

"Then You want me to catch each and every fowl of the earth, the beasts of the field, the insects and amphibia, not forgetting the creeping thing. And when I've caught them, You want me to bring them back here and herd them into the ark. Is that correct?"

"Yes, Noah, that is correct."

And Noah said, "And You want me to do all this in seven days?"

"Yes Noah, that is correct."

And Noah said, "Has anyone ever told You You're out of Your mind?"

And I said, "How would you like to be a cactus?"

And he said, "Well, I can't sit around here chit-chatting to You, I've got animals to catch." And he went on his way praising My name, saying, "God Almighty! What a job!"

After seven days, Noah returned to the ark with two of every animal that lived upon the Earth from the aardvark to the zorro, not forgetting the creeping thing which was called the quug. And people journeyed from far and wide and marvelled, saying, "Typical! Noah's showing off again. If he wants some pets why couldn't he be content with a couple of hamsters?"

But Noah ignored them and led the animals into the ark and gave them food and water, and I commanded the animals to abide on the ark in peace. Hearing My words, the lion lay down with the lamb, the tiger lay down with the kid and the elephant lay down on the quug. Which halved the entire quug population.

And after he had settled the animals, Noah took his family into the ark and as night fell on the seventh day he stood on the deck of the ark with his wife and gazed into the sky and said, "It looks like it might rain."

And she said, "How can you tell?"

And he said, "Because my arthritis is acting up. And because God told me."

And she said, "Nothing like a spot of rain to freshen the place up. Now, do you fancy a nice quug steak for your dinner?"

And lo, I ordained a great and torrential rain. And it rained for forty days and forty nights and everything on the Earth was consumed by the flood waters. And nothing lived on the Earth except those that were in the ark. And for forty days and forty nights the ark bobbed on the surface of the waters.

And for forty mornings Noah looked out of the ark and said, "Guess what? It's still raining."

And for forty mornings Shem said, "Which idiot forgot to pack the seasickness pills?"

And for forty nights Japhet said, "Not quug soup for supper again! Surely God wouldn't miss just one chicken."

And for forty nights Japhet said, "Who's for another game of I Spy? I'll start. I spy with my little eye something beginning with 'R'."

And for forty nights Ham said, "Got it! Rain!"

And for forty nights their wives said to them, "You don't really expect any begatting? Not when I've got one of my migraines. And is it any surprise what with the smell of those animals?"

And for forty days and forty nights Mrs Noah said, "There's nothing like a sea cruise to blow away the cobwebs."

And on the forty-first day, all the rest of them said, "If she says that one more time we'll throw her overboard."

And it was on the forty-first day that I caused the rains to cease. But the ark continued to sail on the waters for another one hundred and fifty days because I was fed up with all their moaning.

And after a while Noah sent forth a raven.

And the raven had a note tied to its leg saying:

Dear God,

Is it all right if we leave the ark?
Yours sincerely,

Noah.

P.S. The weather here is fine, but it rained for the whole of the first forty days and forty nights.
P.P.S. What are we supposed to do with all this animal manure?

And I wrote a note back saying:

Dear Noah,

The waters have not yet abated. Have you any idea how long it takes to drain a whole planet of flood water?

Stay where you are.

You remain my obedient servant,

God,

P.S. Re the manure. You think you've got problems. I've got to find a way to shift a whole planet full of mud.

P.P.S. Don't you know that a raven is not a homing bird?

The raven, not being a homing bird, never returned to the ark. So Noah sent forth a dove with another note saying:

Dear God,

Why didn't You answer our last letter? Can we get off the ark now? We are up to our knees in manure. Also the animals have started begatting. It's getting very crowded, there's not room to swing a cat. So for entertainment, Sharon, Karen, Darren and Warren are having to swing a guinea pig.

We're getting desperately short of food.

Please write soon,

Noah.

P.S. While not questioning Your infinite wisdom, I am beginning to wonder whether bringing two woodworm on board was a good idea.

I sent the dove back and gave it an olive leaf to carry as a sign. Two days later it returned with another message:

Dear God,

The dove just arrived but seems to have lost its letter. The airmail system isn't all it's cracked up to be. However, it did bring an olive leaf for which many thanks. But, frankly, olive leaf pie doesn't go very far among 15 people.

Position is getting desperate. I don't like the way Shem and Japhet keep looking at their brother and saying, "I really fancy a Ham sandwich."

Help!

Noah.

P.S. Since writing the above, Ham has taken matters into his own hands. Instead of sending forth another bird he decided to send forth the one remaining quug by hurling it out of the window to hear if it made a splash or a splat when it landed. After it went splat we concluded that the waters had abated and decided to venture outside.

We seem to have landed on the top of a mountain. Very tricky situation with the ark delicately balanced and in danger of crashing over, especially if the elephants make any unexpected moves. We are fearful for our lives. Please come quickly.

P.P.S. Mrs Noah says the view is very nice.

The trouble with being Me is that people are

always expecting Me to do the impossible. Not unfair, I suppose, because, of course, I can do the impossible.[32]

But I do wish people wouldn't treat Me as though I was some comic book superhero. However, I did answer Noah's plea and made sure the ark was stable by supporting it on My little finger and watched as he checked the animals off.

There were two of everything from the aardvark to the zorro, except for the quug of which there were none. In addition, there were 14 rats, several dozen mice, 23,000 rabbits and countless billion fleas which begat at a rate which surprised even Me. It took days to get them out of My beard; I wish I'd let the wretched things drown. Sometimes I'm too merciful for My own good.[33]

Having disembarked his cargo and set them free to roam the empty vastness of the newly purged Earth,

32. According to what The Author said in footnote 28, regarding blowing in His own ear, it seems that occasionally the impossible defeats even Him. When asked again about this point, He said, "Of course, I can blow into My own ear. I've just never got around to it." Whether this is another of The Author's little jokes is not clear.

33. When asked what the quug, or creeping thing, looked like, The Author said, "It was small, flat and completely covered in turquoise hair. Its nearest existing relative is the fluffy toilet seat cover. It had some extremely distressing personal habits of which emitting a vile odor and attacking dangly bits of unsuspecting males were only two. All-in-all it was no great loss. Though it's a pity about the bandlecroot, a delightful little creature that resembled the koala bear. Unfortunately, being an incredibly slow mover, it was overtaken by all the other animals including the tortoises and arrived at the ark three hours after Noah had locked the doors. A great loss to wildlife documentary makers and soft toy manufacturers."

Noah turned to Me and said, "Well, God, that's that. If it's all the same with You, I'll put my feet up for a while."

And I replied, "Noah your task is not yet complete."

And he said, "Lord, I have already built the biggest ark the world will ever see. I have captured and carefully tended every animal that is on the face of the Earth from the aardvark to the zorro, with the exception of the quug and, according to You, the bandlecroot, although I don't remember ever seeing it. I have endured forty days and forty nights of rain, followed by 150 days and nights plagued by hunger, fear and fleas. Not to mention breaking out in unsightly boils due to my allergy and suffering in other ways from eating rancid quug meat which was not made any better by You neglecting to incorporate adequate toilet facilities in Your blueprints. All this have I done. What do You want me to do now? Move this mountain three feet to the left?"

And I replied, "No, Noah, I want you to go forth and multiply and re-populate the earth."

And Noah looked at me and spake, saying "Oh, is that all! You just want me to father the rest of the human race! Easy-peasy! But may I remind You that in five hundred years I only managed to father Shem, Japhet and Ham. So what do you expect from a 601-year-old man with a low sperm count and a wife who not only suffers from migraines but is approximately four hundred and fifty years past child-bearing age, miracles?"

And I replied, "No, Noah, I'll do the miracles, including turning you into a cactus if you don't get on with the multiplying."

And Noah saw the wisdom in this and called unto him his wife, Norah, saying, "Don't bother to get dressed, we've got some begatting to do."

And she said unto him in return, "Have you been talking to God again?"

"Yes, He wants us to fill the Earth with children."

And she said, "Oh, well, at least it's a nice day for it."

Thus it came to pass that Noah begat and when he wasn't begatting he tended the soil and tried to raise a vineyard.

I was well pleased with My servant and to reward him I gave him the rainbow, saying, "Noah, this is My gift to you."

Noah gazed at the beauty of the rainbow and said, "Very nice, I'm sure, but why couldn't you give me something useful?"

And I replied, saying, "Noah, you are a good man and a faithful servant, but at heart you are a philistine."[34]

"That's all very well," he said, "but what I really want to know is, what I'm supposed to do with a hundred thousand tons of animal manure."

And I told Noah exactly what he could do with it. Which is how Noah raised the most fertile vineyard that ever grew.

He lived for another three hundred years but begat no more children because Mrs Noah made him sleep in a separate room due to the fact that however much he bathed he could never get rid of the smell.

---

34. The Author adds: "But not as big a Philistine as Goliath."

CHAPTER THIRTEEN

Après Le Déluge

There was a great deal of begatting after that and before long Noah's children's children's children started getting ideas above their station. Some, for example, attempted to build the world's first skyscraper in a town called Babel. A stupid idea, particularly as they hadn't yet invented the elevator – nobody was going to pay the rents they were asking when it took three days to climb the stairs from the lobby to the penthouse.

The Bible blames Me for destroying it but you shouldn't take everything The Bible says as gospel, except The Gospels, of course. I never touched the tower; I've got better things to do than go around as a cosmic demolition contractor. Its destruction was due to human greed, the builder was involved in a crooked

SOME OF GOD'S WONDERS

AARDVARK

ZORRO

BANDLECROOT

CREEPING THING
(QUUG)

CACTUS

CERTIFIED VEGETABLE

ADAM

EVE

deal with his brother-in-law – who supplied substandard bricks – and the thing simply collapsed under its own weight. Forty-six estate agents were killed in the accident, so some good came of it.

After the Babelgate scandal, the people involved fled to the four corners of the Earth to escape arrest. They settled in unpopulated areas, set themselves up as vegetables and flourished by cheating each other. However, the law eventually caught up with them and when the police arrived they pretended they didn't understand a word that was being said to them and spoke gibberish in return, which is how the languages of the Earth were invented.[35]

Although I didn't knock over The Tower of Babel, I did, of course, issue a demolition order on Sodom and Gomorrah which were known as The Cities of the Plain, because the people living in them were so physically unattractive. Sadly, their ugliness did not stop them indulging in vile and perverted practices which gave their names to the unnatural acts of sodomy and gomorrahy.[36]

I can't recall whether I've previously mentioned that I am a Merciful God. But even My mercy can only be stretched so far, and having wiped all wickedness

---

35. "Vegetables" are, of course, accountants. This is an interesting revelation about the development of human languages. And may explain why, to this day, most people can't understand a word accountants are saying.

36. "Sodomy" needs no explanation. If it does, consult any standard textbook, good dictionary or average work of pornography. However, the word "gomorrahy" has fallen into disuse. When asked about the act of gomorrahing, The Author was vague but seemed to imply it was a sexual practice involving a goat and a rubber sink plunger.

from The Earth only a few generations previously, I was furious when I discovered that some of you anthropoids were up to your old tricks and, indeed, some new tricks which Adam's great-great-great-etc-grandchildren hadn't discovered. So when one of my contacts in Sodom, a man called Lot – a silly name given by his father who on hearing that he had just had his seventeenth son and twenty-eighth child said, "That's the lot" – told Me what was going on, I decided to investigate for Myself.

Now, obviously, when I descend to Earth I don't go around in a flowing robe that looks like a nightshirt, wearing a halo round My head. It makes Me too conspicuous, especially at night when I am frequently mistaken for a lamppost, especially by dogs. I adopt a different form depending on the situation, sometimes as an anthropoid like yourselves, sometimes as an animal and sometimes as an inanimate object; kindly remember that the next time you stick your chewing gum on the underside of a cinema seat.

For My visits to Sodom and Gomorrah I decided to manifest Myself as an insurance agent, in which guise I could go from house-to-house, from business-to-business, under the pretext of selling My policies.

This was a good ploy because both Sodom and Gomorrah were bustling towns full of small businesses, mostly bars, restaurants and clubs. I went from one den of iniquity to another, each more lascivious and disgusting than the last. And in every place I got the same response. Nobody was interested in insurance – they would soon wish they'd listened more carefully to My sales pitch – and everywhere I went strange men asked Me to dance.

I shall not attempt to describe the appalling sinks

SODOM

AND

GOMORRAH

and stews of Sodom and Gomorrah.[37] Suffice it to say they were like Hell on Earth. The heat, the noise, but worst of all, the people.[38]

I did not need to spend long in these cities of sin to realize that drastic action would have to be taken. Being a Merciful God, before I razed them to the ground I visited Lot to warn him of My decision, but he slammed the door in My face, saying, "I've got all the insurance I need."

37. "Sinks and Stews": the Author is using them in their arcane form, meaning brothels and disorderly houses. Not a reference to either the catering or plumbing found in Sodom and Gomorrah. However, He adds that the hygiene in most of the restaurants did leave much to be desired, especially in Gomorrah where all available sink plungers were being put to another purpose. But the food was surprisingly good. Especially in a little bistro called "Big Boys" which, He recalls, "Served the best mess of pottage I've ever eaten, almost worth Esau selling his birthright for it. I only wish I'd got the recipe before I closed the place down."

38. It seems as though The Author is comparing Hell to a disco. After some thought, He admitted that this wasn't an accurate analogy as some people actually seem to enjoy being crammed into small, hot, stinking holes while being subjected to Grace Jones records played at painfully high volume. He maintains that Hell is even worse than this. A barren, bleak and inhospitable place, where crowds of lost, bewildered souls wander aimlessly through Eternity, gnashing their teeth and bewailing their misfortunes, while being tormented by shrieking devils. In fact, very like the departure lounge of an international airport where the planes never arrive, the restaurants are always closed and the line for the toilets never diminishes and where Grace Jones records are perpetually played at painfully high volume. He said He can't imagine anything worse except listening to Grace Jones records played at painfully high volume on a wet Sunday in November in Belgium.

And I spake unto him, saying, "But I am the man who insured your great-great-etc-grandfather, Noah, against flood."

And he said, "I've heard it all before. Yesterday, a man came round claiming he's sold single glazing to my brother Abraham. A ridiculous idea, putting bits of glass into holes in the wall! And anyway, Abraham lives in a tent!"

And I spake unto him again, saying "Lot, are you insured against fire?"

"Of course, I am."

"And what about brimstone and sulphur?"

And he said, "What about it?"

And I said, "There's going to be a lot of it about and I, the Lord Thy God, have decided to save you from it."

And still he would not listen until I had proved My identity by putting on My halo. And when he finally opened the door, he said, "Forgive me, Lord, for my lack of faith. Sorry I didn't recognize You, but somehow I thought You'd be taller. Now come in quickly before some dog mistakes You for a lamppost."

I entered his humble dwelling and told him to take his wife and his daughters and flee. And I told him that as they fled they must not turn nor look backwards. And when he asked why not, I explained that I didn't like people watching Me as I work.

Lot and his wife and his daughters fled in great haste, and when they were well away from Sodom and Gomorrah, I rained down fire and brimstone and sulphur on to The Cities of the Plain and expunged them from the face of the Earth, together with all who dwelt in them. And very enjoyable it was.

But as the cities were being consumed, Lot's wife turned back, saying, "Lot, because you made us leave so fast, I forgot that I had a cake in the oven." And instantly I turned her into a pillar of salt.

And Lot looked towards Heaven and said, "Why did You do that?"

And I spake, saying, "It is punishment for her disobedience. And if I have any trouble from you, I'll turn you into a pillar of pepper and your daughters into matching condiment pots."

And he said, "All right, all right, there's no need to be ratty, just because You got out of the wrong side of the bed this morning."

And Lot travelled to Zoar where he abided in peace. And he became an object of curiosity in that town because he was the only man who had escaped from Sodom and Gomorrah. And because he was the only man who never took salt on his food, explaining, "You never know who it's been."

CHAPTER FOURTEEN

Out Of Africa

move in mysterious ways My wonders to perform, remember that the next time you see a man crawling on all fours across the fast lane of the highway.

One of the more mysterious ways in which I moved was to disguise Myself as a bush in order to have a chat with Moses. It's a mystery even to Me, can't imagine what possessed Me to do it. But, there I was, manifesting Myself as a rather attractive azalea, waiting for Moses to walk past with his sheep.

It just so happens that azalea bushes were extremely rare in Egypt at that time so you'd have thought that Moses, as he strolled along, would have stopped and said to himself, "That's an unusual shrub, you don't see many azalea bushes in ancient Egypt, I'll take a closer look." Or, at the very least, one of his sheep might have drawn his attention to it by having a nibble at Me and being instantly turned into chops.

But did he see Me? No, he walked straight past. So I had no alternative but to burst into flames. A trifle extreme, I agree, although I have occasionally been tempted to try something similar in restaurants. Even when you possess infinite patience it can be extremely irritating trying to catch a waiter's eye. What has the world come to when God Almighty has to consider flambéing Himself before He can order His post-prandial crème de menthe?

So there I was, burning away and calling, "Moses! Moses!" and he just stood, slack-jawed, staring. And I said, "Don't look so stupid, anybody'd think you'd never seen a burning bush before."

And he said, "Who are You?"

And I said, "I am the Lord Thy God. Who do you think I am, Mickey Mouse?"

And he said, "Who's Mickey Mouse?"

And I said, "Don't bother, it'll take far too long to explain. Now come closer so that I can talk to you without shouting."

And he came closer, and stared in wonder and covered his face, saying, "B-b-bloody Ada, I've singed my eyebrows. Could You turn down the heat a b-b-bit."

Eventually, I managed to make him understand that I had chosen him for a special role. "You are to lead the Israelites out of Egypt and into The Land Flowing With Milk And Honey. And you will give them signs so that they will know you have been appointed by Me."

And Moses said, "B-b-but G-g-god, c-c-can't You g-g-get someone else to t-t-tell them? I've g-g-got th-th-this t-t-terrible st-st-st . . ."

And I said, "All right, I can't wait around all day

while you finish the sentence. Get your brother Aaron to tell them instead."

And Moses said, "Th-th-th-tha ..."

"You're welcome. Now go and tell Aaron what to do."

And Moses told Aaron. And when he'd finished, three days later, Aaron called together all the elders of the Israelites and he showed them the signs that I had given to Moses. First he turned his staff into a serpent. Then he showed them his hand and it was leprous, then he showed them it again and it was healed. Lastly, he poured water on to the ground and it turned to blood.

And the elders were amazed and marvelled, saying, "That's really brilliant! Can I book you for my son's barmitzvah?"

Then Aaron told them how Moses would lead them into The Land Flowing With Milk And Honey. And they said, "We're not going there, it sounds really messy. Imagine the dry cleaning bills!"

But Aaron said, "Is it any worse than being under the whip of the cruel Pharaoh?" And they all agreed it wasn't. All, that is, except Zebediah.[39]

And Aaron said to Moses, "You see, I told you we'd persuade them just as long as you didn't try spinning them that cock-and-bull story about the talking bush."

Moses came to Me, asking what he should do and I told him all that he must do and all that he must say. And Moses went and spake unto Pharaoh saying, "G-g-god has t-t-told m-m-me t-t-to t-t-tell you t-t-to l-l-let m-m-my p-p-people g-g-go". But answer came there none because Pharaoh had fallen alseep. And so Aaron

39. Zebediah, proprietor of The Pyramid Go-Go Bar and Massage Parlor, had some strange tastes.

woke him and briefly repeated what Moses had said and Pharaoh had them thrown out of his palace.

Again they returned. And Moses said, "G-g-god has t-t-told m-m-me ..." And Pharaoh said, "Yes, I know, he told you to tell me to let your people go. But I won't." And so Moses showed him a sign by turning his staff into a serpent. And Pharaoh said, "Seen it! Can't you do something really clever like saw a woman in half?" And they admitted they couldn't, but instead they turned the Nile into a river of blood. And Pharaoh said, "Not bad, but it's been done before. How are you at producing live doves from handkerchiefs?" When they said they hadn't learned that one, Pharaoh had them thrown out again.

And eventually Moses called to Me and said, "L-l-lord, I've d-d-done m-m-my b-b-best t-t-tricks ..."

And I said, "All right, Moses, I know what you're trying to say."

But Moses interrupted Me and said: "If You're so c-c-clever why d-d-don't you c-c-cure m-m-my st-st-stammer?"

So I did. And then I said, "I've had to deal with some stubborn people in My time, but I admit that Pharaoh is the most pig-headed. He's left Me with no alternative but The Plagues."

So I sent a Plague of Frogs, which didn't have the desired effect because the Egyptians were particularly partial to grenouille. And still Pharaoh wouldn't let My people go.[40]

Then I tried plagues of Gnats and Flies, which may not sound too ghastly to you but remember this was years before a really effective aerosol insecticide

40. "Grenouille" is the French for frogs' legs. The Author is showing off again.

had been developed. Still Pharaoh wouldn't change his mind. Then I tried Boils. Nothing. After that, Hail. And finally Locusts.

But still Pharaoh remained implacable. And My wrath was great and I summoned Moses and told him I was going to send the most terrible plague of all but that if he followed My orders to the letter, this plague would not affect the Israelites.

So Moses departed and told the Israelites what I had ordained and, accordingly, they daubed signs on their doors, so that the plague would pass them over.

And on the appointed night I sent the final horror into Egypt – The Plague of Encyclopedia Salesmen.

And so it came to pass that they knocked on the door of every Egyptian house but they did not approach the doors daubed by the Israelites. And faced with this terror Pharaoh called Moses and said unto him, "Okay, I know when I'm beaten. You and your people and herds can go, as long as you take those salesmen with you."

And Moses said, "Rejoice in the name of the Lord, for this is the time of our exodus."

And Pharaoh said, "What does 'exodus' mean?"

And Moses replied, "Look it up in your encyclopedia."

Thus did Moses lead the Children of Israel out of Egypt. Together with the Teenagers of Israel, the Adults of Israel and the Geriatrics of Israel.[41]

41. This account differs significantly from that given in The Bible which maintains that The Author killed the first born son of every Egyptian. When asked, The Author said, "Those Old Testament scribes liked to make Me out as jealous and vengeful. Whereas I am, in fact, a Merciful God. Although it's not something I like to boast about."

CHAPTER FIFTEEN

Parting The Red Sea And Some Other Of My Better Miracles

'm not given to self-doubt; after all, if I expect everyone to have faith in Me, the least I can do is have faith in Myself. But occasionally, in an idle moment, once in every several millennia, I do wonder about My own infinite wisdom. Take Moses, for example; not only did I pick a man with a speech impediment to speak on My behalf, I also chose this man to lead the Israelites out of Egypt and into The Promised Land. A man with absolutely no sense of direction. He couldn't find the toilet in his own house without a map.

No sooner had he started leading the Israelites out of Egypt than he was leading them back into Egypt. So I spake unto him saying, "Moses, turn around again and head for the banks of the Red Sea."

And he said, "Why didn't You tell me we were going to the seaside, I'd have packed my bucket and spade? Now, let me think ... the Red Sea ... that's in the Sahara Desert, isn't it?"

So I sent a column of dust ahead of him to guide his way by day and a column of fire to guide his way by night and erected signposts every mile of the way saying "Red Sea Straight On." As The Children of Israel journeyed onwards, they drove their herds before them, until they came to a sign announcing, "The Red Sea Welcomes Careful Drovers." And then Moses led The Children of Israel to the banks of the Red Sea.

The Israelites clustered round him, saying, "Call these banks? There's nowhere we can change our Traveller's checks!"

And Moses explained that the banks were but the shores of the sea and they said, "Well, this is a nice spot. Why don't we settle here, open some real banks, build condominiums and design robes with little alligators on the breast pockets?"

But those at the back of the line – fifteen miles behind – started sending a message to the leaders, saying, "Pharaoh is coming after us with war chariots, and he looks really annoyed. Maybe he doesn't like the way the encyclopedias were bound in lustrous leather-style vellumette. But what did he expect for the price, hand-tooled morocco?"

When the message reached the head of the line, the Israelites said unto Moses, "On second thoughts, this is a rotten place to build condominiums, we must get out of here. But how will we cross the Red Sea, seeing as there are no boats, nay, not even pedalos?"

And Moses said, "Don't worry, the Lord will part the waters of the sea, so that we can cross."

And I, overhearing this, whispered unto Moses, "How do you expect Me to do that?"

And he said, "You're God, You come up with the answer."

And I said, "I do wish you'd consult Me before making rash promises on My behalf."

And he said, "Why don't You blow on the waters?"

And I said, "I'd remind you that this is the Red Sea, not a cup of hot coffee."

And he said, "You mean You can't do it."

And I said "Of course I can do it, I'm just out of practice at parting seas, that's all."

So I blew mightily upon the Red Sea and the waters parted and the Israelites rushed across. When they were on the opposite bank, I stopped blowing and the waters gushed back again, drowning all the Egyptians and their horses. Which was a bit unfortunate but I was completely out of breath, not being as young as I once was and having a sedentary job in which I don't get enough exercise.

Having been saved from the Egyptians, the Israelites rejoiced, saying, "The Lord has brought us across the Red Sea, which is not as nice as the other side, having less palm trees, a rocky beach and absolutely no water-skiing facilities, but at least there are no Egyptians so I suppose we ought to be thankful for small mercies."

And Moses proposed that they sing "For He's A Jolly Good God" and give three hearty cheers of "Hip, Hip, Hallelujah!" But the Israelites said, "He only deserves two cheers because, after all, we are His chosen people and He was doing no more than His duty. And anyway, we got our shoes wet and who's going to pay for the damage?"

But Miriam took a tambourine and composed a song of praise which went:

Sing to the Lord,
For he is highly exalted.
The horse and its rider
He has hurled into the sea.[42]

And after feasting and rejoicing and recovering from hangovers, and bickering about who was going to pay for the feasting and rejoicing, Moses again led The Children of Israel towards The Promised Land but, turning right instead of left, found himself in the desert. And the Israelites fell to weeping and wailing and gnashing their teeth, complaining, "This is a dreadful place, the landscape is really boring, there are no decent shops and there is nothing to eat or drink. All-in-all, we'd be better off in Egypt where at least, after a hard day building the pyramids, you got a decent chicken noodle soup."

And Moses calmed them, saying, "The Lord will provide."

And I whispered unto him, "Since when was I in the fast food business?"

42. The Author adds: "Not My favorite song about Me, no tune to speak of and the words don't rhyme; it's no wonder that Israel has won The Eurovision Song Contest twice. There have been far better songs praising My name. Without boasting, I've inspired more hit tunes than anyone else. Personally, I prefer something stirring like "God Our Help In Ages Past" or "Abide With Me." Not that many people sing them nowadays, but what can you expect? Religion isn't what it was – talk to most people today about Genesis and they think it's a pop group. And mention My archangel, Gabriel, and they say, "Didn't Phil Collins replace him as the lead singer?"

And he said, "You're supposed to be omnipotent aren't You? All we're asking for is thirty thousand salt beef sandwiches, easy on the mustard; twenty thousand hot pastrami on rye and fifty thousand lox and bagels, half with mayo, half without. And maybe a modest Chablis to wash them down."

And I said, "You'll have what you're given." So I sent them dew to drink and quails and bread from heaven to eat.

And The Children of Israel drank the dew and said, "Well, it slakes the thirst, but Chablis it ain't."

And they caught the quails and consumed them and said, "Call that a square meal? There's hardly enough meat on a quail to keep body and soul together."

And they gathered the bread and ate it and called it "manna", which means "bread from heaven that looks like hailstones and tastes like stale camel blanket."

And I visited Moses and said, "Moses, I have rescued your people from the tyranny of Pharaoh, I have smitten Egypt with plagues, I have delivered you from thine enemies, I have parted the Red Sea and now I have catered for a hundred thousand people at very short notice. And still The Children of Israel complain and moan and bitch. I'm beginning to wonder why I bother with them."

And he spake unto Me, saying, "All these wonders You have wrought because these are Thy chosen people."

And I replied, "Yes, you speak truly. But what I can't work out is why I chose them. Nothing's good enough for them and they're as miserable as sin."

And he said, "Be fair, God, that's just not true. The only thing they don't find miserable is sin."

"Yes, Moses, I was meaning to talk to you about that. There's far too much sinning going on. It's got to stop. I've some Commandments to give you."

And Moses said, "All right, give me a moment to find a pen and paper and I'll jot them down."

"No, Moses, I'm not having you scribbling them on the back of an envelope and losing them. I shall hand down these Commandments on the top of Mount Sinai. Meet Me yonder tomorrow afternoon when I shall descend in glory."

And Moses said, "You are The Lord My God and I will obey. But I think you're making a song and a dance about it."

CHAPTER SIXTEEN

The Eleven Commandments

he next day, at the appointed hour, I descended from Heaven on to the summit of Mount Sinai in a cloud of fire, accompanied by thunder and lightning and the sound of celestial trumpets.

And I spake in a great voice, that caused Sinai to tremble and quake, saying, "Moses! This is The Lord Thy God and here are My Commandments."

And there was an awesome silence.

And I spake again, saying, "Moses! Where the hell are you?"

And three hours later Moses finally arrived, saying, "Sorry I'm late but I must have taken the wrong turn."

And yet again I spake, and My voice was as thunder:

106

"I am The Lord Thy God, which have brought thee out of the land of Egypt, out of the house of bondage."[43]

And Moses said, "Yes, I know all that. Can we skip the introductions and get on to the important bit. And You don't have to shout, I'm not deaf."

And I said, "Moses, it's a good thing I'm a Merciful God or else I would smite thee hip and thigh. I have written My Commandments on these tablets of stone. Read them, understand them and live your life according to them."

And Moses read them and said, "Number One: 'Thou Shalt Have No Other Gods Before Me.' 'Shalt', what sort of word is 'shalt?' "

"Moses, I'm warning you ... hip and thigh."

"I only asked. Number Two: 'Thou Shalt Not Worship False Gods.' As if I would, for God's sake!"

And I answered, "For My sake you will stop saying things like that. You've just broken My Third Commandment: 'Thou Shalt Not Take The Name Of The Lord Thy God In Vain.' "

And Moses said, "I can see this is going to be more difficult than I thought. I didn't realize You were going to be so picky. So far there are an awful lot of 'Thou shalt nots', isn't there any good news? Oh, this is better, Number Four: 'Remember The Sabbath Day, To Keep It Holy.' That's more like it! At least we get the day off every Saturday."

"No, Moses, every Sunday."

"Sunday? How do you work that out?"

"The first day of the week is Monday, which means the seventh day, the day of rest, is Sunday."

And Moses said, "But us Children of Israel have

---

43. The Author is referring to Egypt and not to Zebediah's Pyramid Go-Go Bar and Massage Parlor.

always considered Sunday as the start of the week, which gives us Saturday as the day of rest. It's a bit late to start changing it."

And I spake, saying, "Moses, this is a Commandment of the Lord Thy God. I created the Earth and everything that is upon it in six days, Monday to Saturday inclusive, and rested on the seventh, which was Sunday. And so will The Children of Israel."[44]

"All right, I'll do my best but I'm not guaranteeing anything. The Children of Israel don't like people interfering with their social life. Now let's get on, otherwise I'll be here all night.

"Numbers Five and Six: 'Honor Thy Mother And Father' and 'Thou Shalt Not Commit Murder.' Reasonable enough.

"Number Seven: Oh dear, I'm going to have problems with this. You couldn't tone it down could you?"

And I spake, saying, "When I say 'Thou Shalt Not Commit Adultery', I mean 'THOU SHALT NOT COMMIT ADULTERY'."

"Not even occasionally? Say, three times during your life?"

"NO!"

"Be reasonable. We've been doing it ever since You threw Adam and Eve out of the Garden Center. You told us to go forth and multiply and we couldn't do that without committing adultery."

And I said, "No adultery!"

"Whatever You say. But I'm going to show that clause to Malachi the Lawyer, maybe he can find a loophole."

44. When asked why He allowed The Israelites to defy Him and keep Saturday as The Sabbath, The Author replied, "I'll tell you in Footnote 45."

"There are no loopholes in My Commandments."

"You wait until Malachi starts plea-bargaining on the Murder clause. After listening to him for a few hours, you'll reduce it to Manslaughter, just to get rid of him."[45]

"Moses! I'm tempted to smite thee hip, thigh *and* dangly bits!"

"Enough said! Now, I can't see any problems with Numbers Eight and Nine.[46]

"But this bit in Number Ten, after 'not coveting thy neighbor's ass', telling us we can't covet our neighbor's ox either, that's going to spoil Zebediah's fun.[47]

"Well, if that's the lot, I'll be off to break the bad news to the others."

And I spake, saying, "Thou hast overlooked the words 'Please turn over' on the bottom of the second tablet."

And Moses turned over the tablet and read: "The Eleventh Commandment: 'Thou Shalt Not Turn Thy Sony Walkman Up So Loud That It Annoyeth Others,' What's that supposed to mean?"

45. The Author adds: "I thought I'd have more trouble getting no adultery through, so I traded it in exchange for allowing The Children of Israel to keep Saturday as The Sabbath. Unfortunately, they've been rather more meticulous in taking their day off than they have in obeying Number Seven. Indeed, far too many of them have spent Saturday committing Seven."

46. Commandment Eight is "Thou Shalt Not Steal" and Commandment Nine is "Thou Shalt Not Bear False Witness Against Thy Neighbor." The Author says, "Nine is the Commandment that most people forget, I always compare it to Brad Dexter, the only actor in 'The Magnificent Seven' that most people can't name."

47. Zebediah, ex-proprietor of The Pyramid Go-Go Bar and Massage Parlor, had some *very* strange tastes.

And I told him that in the fullness of time, long after The Children of Israel had found The Promised Land and called it Florida, there would come a blight of noise boxes which would sin against the ears of others. They would spread across the whole earth like a pestilence of McDonald's franchises, and would be more offensive even than parkas, musical doorchimes or Care Bears.

And Moses said, "I don't see how this applies to us. So why don't we do a deal: if The Children of Israel solemnly swear never, ever to break this Commandment, will You drop Adultery?"

"No!"

And with that final word I ascended from Sinai, leaving Moses to contemplate My Commandments.[48]

And he spent forty days and forty nights on the mountain. Two in contemplation and the other thirty-eight trying to find his way back.

48. These Commandments have been published in the order The Author dictated them and not in the order in which they are most commonly broken, which, according to The Author is:
   1. Adultery. (7)*
   2. Taking the name of the Lord in vain. (3)
   3. Theft. (8)
   4. Murder. (6)
   5. Having other Gods before Him (1) *and* Worshipping false Gods, particularly television personalities. (2)
   7. Coveting thy neighbor's ass and other parts of his/her anatomy. (10)
   8. Bearing false witness against a neighbor, particularly after he/she has rejected your caresses of his/her ass and other parts of the anatomy. (9)
   9. Not keeping The Sabbath. (4)
   10. Dishonoring mother and/or father. (5)
   The Author adds that His Commandment regarding the Sony Walkman would have shot straight to Number 3 with a bullet had Moses bothered to pass it on.
   (*) Denotes original position in The Top Ten.

CHAPTER SEVENTEEN

The Land Flowing With Milk And Honey

I had given My great Commandments to Moses so that he should broadcast them throughout the Earth as the rules by which you anthropoids should live your lives, the basis of all your laws and justice. Through him I had revealed to you the truth of all truths.

And having done this I expected you to abide by My Commandments and dwell for ever in peace so that I could retire and live quietly in Heaven, enjoying My infinite old age untroubled by your petty problems. But if there's no peace for the wicked, there's even less for the perfectly righteous.

Hardly had I put My feet up and started on My ornamental macramé than I got a call from Moses. Serves Me right for forgetting to switch My answering machine on.

"Lord," he said, "I've got a problem."

"Moses," I said, "I am fed up with being a cosmic Agony Aunt, the Automobile Association and a deli, all rolled into one. Go somewhere else with your problem."

"I would, Lord, but this involves both of us. Please, don't hang up until You've heard what I've got to say."

And so, in My infinite patience, I let him speak.

"It's like this: I returned from Sinai to The Children of Israel. And they gathered round me, asking, 'What kept you on the mountain for the past forty days and forty nights?'

"And I said, 'I've been taking a skiing holiday. What do you think kept me? I have been speaking with The Lord and He has vouchsafed me His Commandments which are contained in these tablets of stone.'

"And they said, 'Why are you clutching your groin?'

"And I said, 'Because I've given myself a hernia lugging these great tablets of stone down the mountain.'

"And the Israelites said, 'What are these Commandments?'

"And I recited Your Commandments to them. After I'd finished it went very quiet and so I asked them what they'd been doing while I was away."

"So, Moses," I asked, "what had they been doing?"

"Well, Lord, it seems they'd been having a bit of a party."

"So?"

"So, apparently they had this idea of building a golden calf and celebrating round it and what with the drink, well, one thing led to another and I'm afraid, Lord, that a few things got broken."

"What got broken?"

"At least seven Commandments. Eight, if you include Zedediah and the ox."

So saying, Moses threw himself to the ground and begged My forgiveness, saying "I know they have done wrong and deserve to be punished, but I am pleading with You to spare them. And, in fairness, not one of them broke Your Eleventh Commandment."

And I was moved by his pleas and spake gently unto him saying, "Moses, contrary to what some people believe, I am a Merciful God, and therefore I will not strike down the Israelities with thunderbolts, nor will I rain fire and brimstone upon their heads, nor even turn them into jumbo packs of superior table salt. But they must be punished for transgressing My laws, so I have decided that henceforth the Israelites will carry with them a terrible burden. I will place My Curse on one child in every four. And from this day hence until all eternity every fourth child of the Israelites will be reviled and despised and even his own kith and kin will flee from him, shouting, 'Truly this is the most horrendously boring person we have ever had the misfortune to meet'."

And thus did I place My Curse on the Children of the Children of Israel so that even unto this day, one in four of them is a Certified Vegetable.[49]

So Moses returned to the Israelites and told them My decision and there was much weeping and wailing

---

49. The Author adds that, in retrospect, He thinks this punishment might have been too severe, not only to the Israelites and their descendants but also to the rest of us. But He didn't envisage Certified Accountants becoming as numerous as they are. "I wish I'd told them to go forth and subtract."

and each of them beat their breast and gnashed their gums.[50]

But I hardened My heart against them and to show I meant business I ordained that one in four should immediately become Certified Vegetables and be put to work conducting a census, counting the number of able-bodied men before they resumed their journey towards The Land Flowing With Milk And Honey.

And Moses reported back to Me when the census was taken, saying that the total number of men was 603,567 and that they were split into thirteen families who became The Thirteen Tribes of Israel. And then Moses said, "Lord, why in Your infinite wisdom, did You make us spend three months counting all 603,567 able-bodied men?"[51]

And I answered, saying, "Merely a whim. Sometimes I just enjoy acting like God."

50. Dental hygiene was still in its infancy.

51. For the record the figures broke down thus:
    Tribe of Reuben: 46,500; Tribe of Simeon: 59,300; Tribe of Gad: 45,650; Tribe of Judah: 74,600; Tribe of Issachar: 54,400; Tribe of Zebulun: 57,400; Tribe of Joseph: 40,500; Tribe of Manasseh: 32,200; Tribe of Benjamin: 35,400; Tribe of Dan: 62,700; Tribe of Asher: 41,500; Tribe of Naphtali: 53,400; Tribe of Trevor: 17.
    There is no mention in the Old Testament of the 13th and smallest Tribe of Israel, The Tribe of Trevor. The Author explains that Trevor was a close relative of Moses and shared his lack of a sense of direction. When the other tribes set off for The Promised Land, Trevor went in the opposite direction and he and his family were never seen again. They became known as The Lost Tribe of Israel. According to The Author, they wandered aimlessly across the globe for a thousand generations until they finally arrived in The Promised Land in 1979. But due to the exorbitant rents in Miami Beach, they moved on again.

And once more Moses led the 603,567 men and their wives and their children towards The Land Flowing With Milk And Honey. And throughout the journey the 603,567 men and their wives and their children each said, "I think we should go this way" and "No, I'm certain we should go that way" and "I know we've been past this rock at least fifteen times" and "When you've seen one desert, you've seen them all!" and "All I say is, this Land Flowing With Milk And Honey better be something special."

And thus they travelled for forty long and weary years. And as they went each of them wept and wailed and beat their breast. And when they tired of that, they beat Moses's breast and his head and his dangly bits.

At the end of forty years, Moses came to Me and said, "Lord, for forty long and weary years I have led The Children of Israel through the desert and still I cannot find The Land Flowing With Milk and Honey. Tell me where I am going wrong."

And I spake unto Moses, saying, "Moses, for forty years you have been reading the map upside down."

And Moses said, "So where is The Land Flowing With Milk and Honey?"

And I pointed westwards and said, "See that river? That is The Jordan and beyond Jordan is Canaan and that is The Land Flowing With Milk and Honey."

And Moses said, "How far is that from here?"

And I said, "About three hundred yards."

And he said, "Well, I'll be damned."

And he died.

But before he expired he spake his last words unto Me, saying, "Lord there is something I've always meant to tell You, but could never pluck up my courage to say."

And I said, "Tell Me now Moses."

And he looked at Me and with his dying breath he uttered these words, "You're a lot shorter than I imagined You would be."

So it came to pass that the mantle of Moses passed to Joshua. And after he had let the seams out, raised the hem and had a small alligator embroidered on the breast pocket, he took command.

Thus it was Joshua who finally led The Children of Israel across the River Jordan and into Canaan which was The Land Flowing With Milk and Honey.

And when they arrived there The Children of Israel fell to the ground and kissed the earth. And they raised their heads to the sky and, with one voice cried, "This earth tastes like earth. So where's the milk? Where's the honey?"

And I spake with a great voice, saying unto The Children of Israel, "There was milk, there was honey. But research will prove they are packed with cholesterol, so to protect your health I am giving you The Land Flowing With Mineral Water And High-Fiber Bran."

And The Children of Israel set to weeping and wailing and threatening to sue Me for false pretenses. And they shrieked, "For forty long and weary years we have journeyed through the desert just for this!" But I ignored them and left them to their misery.

You know, sometimes I really love being Me.

CHAPTER EIGHTEEN

Prophet And Loss

had achieved all I set out to do. I had created the world in six days, I had populated it and I had finally led My Chosen People into The Land Flowing With Mineral Water And High-Fiber Bran. Having done all this, and tired of being a cosmic au pair to The Children of Israel, I left them to get on with it, while I finally enjoyed a quiet life in Heaven with My macramé.

Well, not that quiet because The Children of Israel kept asking Me to pop back to help them out of the various messes they got themselves into. Quite soon after Joshua had assumed leadership, he found himself outside Jericho and didn't know how to take the town. So I told him to march his men round the city while trumpeters blew blasts on their ram horns.

The Bible says that after the trumpeting the walls just tumbled down. Not quite how it happened.[52]

Whatever their virtues – and the Israelites must have had some, though they don't spring easily to mind – they were not great trumpeters. To be honest – and I can't be anything else – they had no musical ability whatsoever; personally I'd prefer to listen to cats being eviscerated alive than suffer an evening of hearing them murder "Hava Nagila", which was the only tune they knew. And not one of My favorites, I wish I'd made The Twelfth Commandment: "Thou Shalt Not Under Any Circumstances Ever Play, Sing or Otherwise Perform 'Hava Nagila'."[53]

Be that as it may, they started marching around Jericho trumpeting "Hava Nagila" and the Jerichoans – who had an ear for music – were so appalled by the

52. The Author adds: "Some of these Old Testament stories should be taken with a pinch of Lot's wife."

53. The Author indicated that He has other Commandments to be passed on including:
 • Thou Shalt Not Snigger When Thy Neighbor's Card Is Swallowed By The Money Machine.
 • Thou Shalt Not Slam Down The Receiver Before Leaving A Message On Thy Neighbor's Answering Machine.
 • Thou Shalt Not Covet Thy Neighbor's Parking Space.
 He also said He is considering reducing The Deadly Sins to six: "I'm thinking of dropping Sloth as it is unfair to a perfectly harmless, if very boring, animal, which is neither sinful nor deadly. Unless, of course, it happens to fall out of a tree and drop on your head."
 When we questioned Him about this He said, "That's one of My best jokes." He then told us that if we didn't find it funny we should go forth and multiply ourselves, although not exactly in those words.

120

racket that they started protesting by booing, hissing and throwing rotten greengroceries. When these ran out, they threw whatever else they could lay their hands on, including the bricks in the walls of the city. And so they stupidly demolished their own fortifications.[54]

I felt quite sorry for the Jerichoans; not only were they the cause of their own downfall, they were also rotten shots. Not one brick came anywhere near an Israelite and all the trumpeters lived to play another day. Ultimately, their appalling atonal music influenced such composers as Stockhausen. (Although his works never brought the house down.)

Between errands like this I kept only a watching brief as the Israelites spent the next centuries squabbling and fighting amongst themselves and with anyone else. The Israelites were their own worst enemies, except, perhaps, for the Philistines and the Romans. They never learned. Look at Samson, would he listen when I advised him that a nice, well-educated Israelite boy should never marry a hairdresser?

And so it went on throughout The Old Testament,

54. It seems the bricks for the walls of Jericho were supplied by the same man who won the contract for The Tower of Babel. After their great victory The Israelites marched in to the ruins of Jericho only to find that several dozen estate agents had got there first and already had planning permission to develop the site into a drive-in hyperstore with parking for fifteen hundred chariots.

they ignored My every warning. I kept sending down
My prophets and they just refused to heed them. So in
the end I gave up and scrapped My prophet-sharing
scheme.[55]

55. The Author says He knows this is an old joke – about six
    thousand years old, to be precise – but it still amuses Him.
    And, indeed, it caused the publishers a great deal of mirth.
    When asked His views about modern prophets The Author
    replied: "I am a Merciful God, as I think I may have once
    said, but I find it hard to be patient with those who
    proclaim. 'I have found God!' As though they'd discovered
    Me in a Lost Luggage office like some umbrella carelessly
    left on a train.
        "And I do find it difficult to be Merciful to those who set
    themselves up as My spokesmen on Earth. Never trust
    anyone who says that I speak through them. I am not some
    sort of cosmic ventriloquist. And even if I was, I'd be very
    fussy about up whom I put My hand."

CHAPTER NINETEEN

Upstairs, Downstairs

A t last I was able to spend more time at home which by now was getting quite full. After so many eons of living alone it was nice to welcome some congenial companions.

As you would expect, we run a pretty tight membership policy. We don't let any old riff-raff in, so it's no good knocking three times on The Pearly Gates and saying, "Come on, Peter, open up! John Paul II sent me and said to give You his regards." We must have a thousand people try that one every day and all are briskly turned away.

We don't, of course, have anything as vulgar as bouncers – not like Downstairs where they have a score of them throwing people in. But nobody gets past St Peter without being sponsored by at least two saints and seconded by a couple of popes.

Not that every pope is a member here. Frankly, I don't know how some of them got the job, especially in the Middle Ages when some very undesirable individuals managed to persuade others that they were My Representative on Earth. The trouble is, I don't have any say in who gets elected as Pope. Now, I'm not saying that John Paul II isn't a good man – he is, even if he does rather overdo the speaking in tongues; making long speeches in a dozen different languages is suspiciously like showing-off – but if I'd had My way I'd have thought twice before electing a pontiff who seems to be unnaturally fond of kissing tarmac.

A strange habit but harmless enough, I suppose, and vastly preferable to the proclivities of some of his predecessors who did not confine their affection to airport runways and seemed to think they had to test every Deadly Sin personally before warning their flock against them. We don't want that sort of person up here and most of them didn't get within a stone's throw of The Pearly Gates – just as well because there's nothing that does a Pearly Gate more damage than having stones thrown at it.[56]

Over the millennia we've tried to keep Heaven

---

56. When asked to name His favorite pontiffs, The Author said, "There have been 262 of them so it's very difficult to compile My Top of the Popes. For Me, St Peter, who was the very first, is still Number One. But I have trouble remembering some of them. After all, there were fourteen called Clement and twenty-three called John, most confusing, though I'm very fond of John XXIII, who is very charming. But who was Deusdedit? And what possessed one of them to call himself Donus? Sounds like a Turkish kebab." When reminded that St Deusdedit (a.k.a. Adeodatus I) was pope from 615–619 and that Donus held the post from 676–678, The Author told the editor, "Nobody likes a Know-it-all."

exclusive. Very few people have even had a glimpse of it, which is probably why so much nonsense has been talked about the place. It's not all fluffy clouds and angels playing harps; there are almost no clouds because most of us like to sunbathe the whole year round and quite a few of the angels now play synthesizers. We move with the times although, as I said to Ludwig only the other day, I vastly prefer "Rock of Ages" to the age of rock![57]

That little *bon mot* amused the dear old man, who doesn't approve of this new music at all, in fact he recently begged Me to make him deaf again. I think he was joking, although it's difficult to tell with him. He's got a kind heart, though. He spends hours with Schubert suggesting ways in which he might finish his 8th Symphony.

Mozart, on the other hand, has taken to the new technology like a duck to water and has written a rock opera called "Cosi Fan Tutti Frutti." Not altogether to My taste; give Me something a little more traditional like "The Hallelujah Chorus" – I'm afraid that even a God as modest as Me likes to hear His name being exalted – but it's very popular with the younger seraphim. Call Me old-fashioned but I do wish they wouldn't wear jeans, even ones with My son's name written on them. No, I may be a fuddy-duddy but I still like to see seraphim dressed in traditional gossamer, at least while they're working.

The nice thing about Heaven, as some of you may find out, although I doubt it, is that it's whatever you want it to be. Everyone has their personal Paradise. My

57. Ludwig van Beethoven. It would seem The Author is as prone to name-dropping as the rest of us.

own little bit of Heaven is just a cosy corner which I haven't changed much since I created the place, although Michelangelo did redecorate the ceiling. Very nice too but a bit elaborate. Being a God of simple tastes, I'd have been quite happy with a bit of lining paper and a couple of coats of lacquer. Not that I said anything – you know how temperamental geniuses can be.

Perhaps you don't but that's because you haven't been up here where you can hardly turn round without bumping into one. And, of course, most of you won't have the chance unless you're very, very righteous.

Contrary to popular opinion, the vast majority of you probably won't go Downstairs either. It's possible I've already mentioned that I'm a Merciful God. And as such, I don't like to think of people spending the rest of Eternity in The Other Place unless they really are beyond redemption. I like to believe there's a little good in all of you, so try not to disappoint Me. I make sure that each case is judged carefully and if I feel that a sinner may genuinely repent, I dispatch him or her to Limbo.

There are some serious misconceptions about Limbo. Most people seem to think it's like some eternal dentist's waiting room, full of old magazines and dusty cacti with some nasty treatment to follow. Not to mention an exorbitantly high bill to pay. (I do apologize for teeth, they are so unreliable. I'll look again at their design when – I mean if – I ever think of scrapping you anthropoids and starting anew.)

Nothing could be further from the truth. It's a very pleasant place, attractive and comfortable without being opulent. I send people there to mend the errors of their ways, to revitalize their souls and uplift their

spirits. It's a bit like a Health Farm with spiritual jacuzzis. After a while the clients emerge looking, feeling and, most important, behaving better and if they've thoroughly cleansed their souls, they may even become probationary members of Heaven. Sadly, though, there are some who won't follow orders and I'm afraid that, with great reluctance, I have to kick them Downstairs.

I won't dwell on The Other Place in detail; if you really want to find out what it's like just try stealing this book.[58]

Suffice to say that it is indescribably vile, filthy, stinking, unbearably hot and crammed with the most loathsome, despicable and genuinely monstrous people. Also the food leaves a lot to be desired. It is a hundred million times worse than the very worst thing you can imagine. Yes, even worse than watching "The Price is Right" for all eternity.

I keep My visits to a minimum, just popping down to complain when they're being unusually noisy or when they aren't stoking the furnaces sufficiently high and it affects My central heating system.

Otherwise I try to avoid the place because I don't see eye-to-eye with Satan. He's always been an awkward customer. I remember thinking he was a wrong 'un when he was a child and I caught him trying to pull the wings off a cherub.

In those days he was living up here and had he mended his ways he might have done quite well. Some thought he had the makings of an archangel. But his

---

58. The Author wishes us to point out that He is much too merciful to impose such a sentence for shop-lifting. But warns that anyone who does try to steal this book is liable to spend the rest of their days in a dentist's waiting room as a cactus.

problem was ambition. He got ideas above his station and started thinking he could do better than Me! He used to go around telling the other angels that I was getting too old for the job and trying to tempt them to join him in a boardroom coup against Me.

In the end I had it out with him, face-to-face. I told him that if he didn't change he would regret it.

He said, "Do your worst, you stupid old fool."

And I said, "Satan, being a Merciful God, I don't want to do My worst although I am sorely tempted to."

And he said, "Go on, just this once, give in to temptation."

And I said, "If you think that I would give in to temptation, you can go to Hell."

No sooner had the words left My lips than there was an almightly explosion and he disappeared in a pillar of fire and sulphur. Sometimes I forget My own omnipotence.

He's been in charge of Hell ever since. And when he's not tormenting lost souls, he goes out on recruitment drives, wandering the Earth trying to convince gullible fools to buy a Time Share in Hades.

CHAPTER TWENTY

The End Of The Word[59]

’m drawing towards the end of this little volume of My memoirs. And looking back over all the trials and tribulations of a long and eventful existence, I find I have no regrets. Except, perhaps, that I would have liked to have been taller.

The story isn't complete. It will never be complete because I am Infinite. I have other stories to tell. For example, I have barely touched on My son's story, simply because I have very little to add to what is said in The New Testament.

I also have stories to tell of other life-forms in other

---

59. When we asked The Author if this was a misprint for "The End Of The World", He waxed wrathful and said, "Why do you question every tiny thing I do? The Lord Thy God does not make typing errors. I am omniscient. If I write 'The End of The Word', I mean it."

worlds in other galaxies in other universes. And some day I may be persuaded to put pen to paper and relate them. Though I'll probably use other publishers. These, if I may be allowed a personal observation, have been unnecessarily over-zealous in questioning some of My facts.[60]

As for My holy ghost writer, well, we finally managed to establish some sort of rapport and he will doubtless spend the rest of his life quite happily as a cactus. In fact, I know he will because I am omniscient.[61]

Omniscience is all very well but it can be a curse. For a start, it ruins My birthday every year because I know in advance what presents I'm going to receive.[62]

Mind you, I'd know that even if I wasn't omniscient because they are the same every year – new pyjamas, a flowing robe and thonged leather sandals – as Gabriel says, "What can you give the God who has everything?"

He says it every year, and I know he's going to say it. And every year I want to say, "Forget about those terrible sandals, why don't you give Me a pair of Reeboks?" But I don't.

And every year he says, "Guess what I've made especially for You!"

60. We were going to question the veracity of this statement, but decided against it.

61. The last time we looked, the holy ghost writer seemed quite content on the windowsill and is being well cared for by one of our secretaries. However, we are now faced with the unique problem of paying royalties to a potted plant but our company's Certified Vegetable is working on it.

62. The Author does not actually have a birthday as He wasn't actually born. However, He holds a celebration on February 30th each year which is a Sunday.

And every year I say, "You've baked Me an archangel cake!"

And every year, he says, "Surprise! Surprise! I've baked You a fruit cake!"

And every year I know he has but I hate to spoil his fun.

And every year he says, "Well, Lord, how old are You this year?"

And every year I say, "Gabriel, I stopped counting after the first thirty-nine millennia."

And every year he says, "I must say You don't look a day over thirty-five thousand!"

And we all laugh.

Then we play a game of "Trivial Pursuit" and every year I win. And every year Gabriel gets grumpy and says, "It's not fair, being omniscient You know all the answers."

And every year I say, "I knew you were going to say that."

And every year he says, "Well, just remember, nobody likes a Know-it-all."

And every year I pretend to get cross and say, "Gabriel! You shouldn't talk to the Lord Thy God like that. I've half a mind to send you Downstairs for the rest of eternity."

And every year he says, "But You're not going to."

And every year I say, "Give Me one reason why I won't."

And every year he says, "Because You're a Merciful God."

And every year I say, "Sometimes, Gabriel, I think you're nearly as omniscient as I am."

And we laugh.

132

SIZE: VAST
AVE A GOOD DAY, GOD! HAVE A GOOD DAY, GOD! HAVE A GO
APPY BIRTHDAY, GOD! HAPPY BIRTHDAY, GOD
VE A HEAVENLY BIRTHDAY, GOD! HAVE A HEAVENLY BIRT

It's the same every year, year in, year out, through infinity. I suppose some of you might think it's boring but it suits Me.

Perhaps omniscience does bring its problems, but I always knew it would so I don't complain. In fact, I complain about very little which is quite remarkable considering how much trouble you anthropoids have caused Me over the millennia.

You're the most disputatious, vexatious and ungrateful of all My creations. Day after day, year after year, century after century you have let Me down. You've gone your own way, ignored My teaching, ridiculed My prophets, abused My priests, waged war and committed atrocity in My name. And I know you'll never change.

Can you wonder that there have been occasions when you've tried even My infinite patience so sorely that I've thought seriously about rubbing you all out and starting again? But call Me sentimental if you like or put it down to the fact that I'm growing mellow in My old age but I haven't yet been so aggravated that I've clicked My fingers and turned you and your little Earth back to the dust from whence I made you.

And perhaps I'm also getting a little bit lazy. Because I start to think, "Why should I go to all the trouble and expend all the energy required to blow them to smithereens when they are quite capable of doing it for themselves? And certainly stupid enough to succeed."

Be assured, one day your microscopic world will disappear. And, being omniscient I know the question you are asking: When will the end of the world come?

I alone know the exact day, hour, minute and second of Armageddon. And I could reveal it here. But

My omniscience shows me the awful effect the news would have on you.

I know the panic, agony and despair that would engulf you. And, in my Infinite wisdom, I have decided to spare you that unbearable anguish.

I also know that if I revealed the date to you, you'd rush straight out and bet money at enormous odds, certain you'll win a fortune. But, money won't buy you happiness. Indeed, on the day that your bet comes up, it won't buy you anything at all, not even a decent burial.

So I've decided I'm not going to tell you when your world will end. Let's just say that your little Earth, like My story, is to be continued ...

And even though I may have mentioned it in passing before, I am, I think you will agree, a Merciful God.

Amen.

God

You can get up off your knees now.

CHAPTER ONE

In The Beginning ...

n most autobiographies the subject starts at the beginning, but in My case that's tricky. I have no beginning. And for that matter, I have no end. I'm Infinite. So it makes starting the story difficult. Not to mention ending it. In theory this book could continue indefinitely which ... Haven't I written this bit before? That's the trouble with being Infinite, you never know whether something's already happened or is about to happen ...

BY THE SAME AUTHOR

'God On Gardening'

'God Housekeeping – How To Have
a Heavenly Home'

'Kitchen Miracles – Including 101 Ways
To Cook a Quug'

'Build Your Own Universe'

'The Joy Of Begatting' (co-author, The Holy Ghost)

'Begatting, The Do's And Don'ts'

'The Book Of Judgment'
(co-author, The Recording Angel)

'Monroe and Me – My Memories of Marilyn'

INDEX

Figures in *italic* denote illustrations

BIBLEOGRAPHY

In writing this volume The Author occasionally consulted the following sources:

THE BIBLE, Old Testament, various authors including Amos, Daniel, Esther, Ezekiel, Ezra, Habakkuk, Haggai, Hosea, Isaiah, Jeremiah, Job, Joel, Jonah, Joshua, Leviticus, Malachi, Micah, Nahum, Nehemiah, Obadiah, Ruth, Samuel, Zechariah, Zephaniah and Trevor. The latter's work is known as The Lost Book of The Old Testament as Trevor mislaid it somewhere in Canaan during his lifetime's wanderings.

THE BIBLE, New Testament, various authors including Matthew, Mark, Luke, John, Peter, Paul and Mary.

THE RED SEA SCROLLS, the soon-to-be-discovered Book of Trevor. The Author found Chapter 28 – 'From Ur To Thur And Back Again' – particularly misleading.

'THE NOAH LETTERS', written by Noah and his wife Norah to The Author. Also 'The Noah Postcards'. In The Author's own collection.

'ORNAMENTAL MACRAMÉ MADE EASY' by Vera Swain.

ALSO RECOMMENDED
'THE CARE AND PROPAGATION OF CACTI'
by Laurens Wilp

ADDENDA

The following are late additions to The Author's original manuscript.

ANCHOVY
The use of, as a cure for bunions. Apply to affected part. If symptoms still persist, consult a chiropodist.

ANGELS
In an attempt to settle the age-old theological dispute we asked The Author exactly how many angels could stand on a pinhead. He replied, "I am The Lord Thy God and not 'The Guinness Book of Records'."

BUGGROM
A suburb of Sodom, which suffered the same fate.

COCKTAIL ONION
Original inspiration for the planet Dandropy in the thirty-ninth galaxy of the fourth universe, turn left after Nibolt and ask again.

DANDROPY
Don't bother asking directions at Nibolt. Since this book was written Dandropy has ceased to exist.

JEHOVAH'S WITNESSES
The Author requests that they kindly desist from knocking on The Pearly Gates attempting to sell him 'The Watch Tower'.

MABBLE
Small barnacle-like creature found clinging to the bottom of the Ark after it had landed on Mount Ararat. Unable to live outside water and so became instantly extinct.

ORNAMENTAL MACRAMÉ
Since writing the manuscript, The Author has decided that the ornamental macramé hanging basket is a worse plague than boils and wishes every reference to it to be expunged from this work. Unfortunately, His decree came too late to be incorporated into this edition.

SAINT BARRY
Barry Felt will be canonized by Pope Sade in 1997 and created the Patron Saint of Video Producers.

ZYGL
The Author's original name for rubber overshoes.

ERATTA

There are no eratta as The Author doe not make mistakes.

ERRATUM

'Eratta' should be spelt 'errata'. The Publisher apologizes for this errer.